Lucie Delarue-Mardrus

AMANIT

Translated and with an Introduction by
Brian Stableford

THIS IS A SNUGGLY BOOK

ISBN: 978-1-64525-077-7

AMANIT

LUCIE DELARUE-MARDRUS (1874-1945) was born in Honfleur in Normandy, the youngest of the six daughters of an advocate. In 1900 she married the Orientalist Joseph-Charles Mardrus (1868-1949), a marriage which endured until 1913, but the union was confused from the outset by Lucie's apparent preference for women as sexual partners. She was a member of Natalie Barney's coterie of female poets and was rumored to have had affairs with more than one of them. A prolific author, she produced more than seventy books, including the collection of poetry *Ferveur* (1908) and the novels *L'Acharnée* (1910) and *Amanit* (1929).

BRIAN STABLEFORD's scholarly work includes *New Atlantis: A Narrative History of Scientific Romance* (Wildside Press, 2016), *The Plurality of Imaginary Worlds: The Evolution of French roman scientifique* (Black Coat Press, 2017) and *Tales of Enchantment and Disenchantment: A History of Faerie* (Black Coat Press, 2019). He has translated more than three hundred volumes from the French, mostly in the genres of *roman scientifique*, *contes de fées* and Romantic and Symbolist fiction. His recent fiction includes the visionary science fiction novel *The Revelations of Time and Space* (2020) and its sequel *After the Revelation* (2021); the last in his long series of "Tales of the Genetic Revolution," *The Elusive Shadows* (2020); and the comedy fantasy *Meat on the Bone* (2021), all published by Snuggly Books.

CONTENTS

INTRODUCTION

*A*MANIT by Lucie Delarue-Mardrus was first published in three parts as numbers 190-192 in the
Petite Illustration series of booklets, issued in association
with the periodical *L'Illustration* in 1929; it was then
reprinted in a single volume by Fasquelle, also in 1929.
The name Amanit had been used by the author twice
before, in the course of her many fictional contributions
to the daily newspaper *Le Journal*, for which she worked
regularly as a journalist from 1906 until her death in
1945. Its first use was in the context of a loosely-knit serial, "La Princesse en Balade" [The Traveling Princess], the
fourth episode of which, individually titled "La Momie
consolatrice" (*Le Journal*, 10 February, 1911), features
Amanit and is here translated as "The Consolatory
Mummy." The second employment of the name was in a
short story published in the "Contes du Journal" section
of the newspaper, "Le Secret d'Amanit" (*Le Journal*, 6
March 1923), here translated as "Amanit's Secret."
The first of the three items, obviously based on one of
the author's numerous visits to Egypt—the character of
"Princesse Patricia" had been used before in stories seem-

7

ingly based on her own experiences, and reflects the fact that when she first became prominent in Parisian society as a "professional beauty" she was nicknamed "Princesse Amande"—features the real Amanit: a mummy in the museum of Cairo bearing the label "The Lady Amanit, priestess of Hathor," then speculatively dated to 1900 B.C. or thereabouts (more recent research suggests a date some eight hundred years later.)[1] The second item applies the name to a different, entirely fictitious, mummy.

Neither of the Amanits of the early stories is the same person as the eponymous character of the novella, but the reuse of the name does signify a link of sorts between the three items, which is more complicated than the simple fact that all three stories are derived from Egyptological discoveries and their imaginative spinoff. The reactions of Princesse Patricia in the first story and the unnamed narrator of the second—also an *alter ego* of the author—illustrate feminine preoccupations not unconnected with the subtext of *Amanit*, and to the author's conception of the story, although the primary focus of the novella is an issue particular to it. There is, therefore, some utility in reproducing all three stories for the purpose of contextualization.

Because *Amanit* is framed as a mystery story, in such a way that its central concern is not made explicit until the revelatory climax, it would be difficult to discuss its

---

1 The real Amanit obtained a curious celebrity in 2011, when she was one of 52 mummies employed in a medical study of atherosclerosis in ancient Egypt. The name was also borrowed, in slightly distorted form, for the "Princess Ahmenet" featured in the 2017 movie *The Mummy*.

theme here without providing a damaging "spoiler," so I shall leave a specific commentary on its content to an afterword and restrict my further introductory remarks to some biographical details relative to the author and a few suitably oblique observations about the relationship of *Amanit* to the general context of the author's writings.

Lucie Delarue was born in Honfleur in Normandy in 1874, the youngest of the six daughters of an advocate; although the family relocated to Paris when she was six years old, they revisited Normandy routinely, and Lucie retained a strong nostalgic attachment to the region. Later in life, she served as a nurse in Honfleur during the Great War, and eventually, while still living and working in Paris, she acquired a property there. She eventually died in the town, in difficult circumstances, overwhelmed by debts run up and long sustained by a slightly extravagant lifestyle.

Delarue-Mardrus recorded in her autobiographical writings that her older sisters teased her a great deal when she was a child, with ostentatious contempt, and the children who feature as protagonists in many of her short stories and novels, the termination of whose childhood illusions is routinely featured as the most poignant cruelty of her *conte cruel* endings, are invariably described as being "different", by virtue of being more imaginative than their fellows and more inclined to be self-indulgent in the uses of their imagination. She considered, however, that she had obtained a due revenge on her prosaic sisters when her physical youth became an advantage and she acquired a reputation in her late teens and twenties for exceptional beauty, becoming a "princesse" of the Parisian high society popularly known as Tout-Paris.

In no hurry to give up her renown as a "professional beauty", she did not marry until 1900, to the Orientalist Joseph-Charles Mardrus (1868-1949), a great traveler, a lover of flowers and precious stones, and an enthusiastic photographer—all interests that his wife shared, and which assisted her to further her burgeoning career as a journalist; the couple's frequent visits to North Africa provided raw material for many of her short stories and much of her non-fictional reportage. Although the marriage endured until 1913, it seems to have been confused from the outset by Lucie's preference for women as sexual partners; she was a member of Natalie Barney's coterie of female poets and was rumored to have had affairs with more than one of them, with the knowledge and apparent approval of her husband, whose esthetic appreciation of her allegedly extended to not wanting her to have children lest it spoil her figure—although reading between the lines of her fiction suggests that it might have been at least as much her anxiety as his. At any rate, one of the constant preoccupations of fiction based on her actual travels and encounters—including "La Momie consolatrice"—is a quasi-neurotic fear of aging and the fading of beauty: a preoccupation that is by no means irrelevant to the bizarre plot of *Amanit*, albeit in an oblique fashion that makes an interesting contrast with "La Momie consolatrice." That contrast is partly reflective of the fact that in February 1911 the author was only thirty-six, whereas in 1929 she was well over fifty and her pre-Great War career as a professional beauty must have seemed almost as remote as ancient Egypt.

When Delarue-Mardrus began writing for *Le Journal* in 1906 she was the first female writer recruited to supply material on a regular basis to the "Contes du Journal" feature and remained the only one; although Gérard d'Houville (Marie de Régnier) also supplied two stories to the slot in 1907 she never became a regular. Delarue-Mardrus supplied thirty-five distinctive short stories to the paper before switching to the option followed by several of her predecessors and using the slot to publish "series" of stories that were, in essence, serial novels written and published on a more leisurely schedule than the newspaper's daily feuilleton serials. Most of her contributions from 1908 onwards were serialized novels and novelettes, often consisting of loosely-knit assemblages of episodes, after the fashion of "La Princesse en balade."

Translations of those first thirty-five stories, many of which are flamboyantly fantastic, can be found in the Snuggly Books volume *The Last Siren and Other Stories*; they form a distinct set, not merely because it was more than two years before she began intruding independent short stories into the series again, but because the editors of the newspaper eventually altered the required wordage of stories written for the slot, so that they became much shorter and slighter, after the curt fashion of "Le Secret d'Amanit." The intervention of the Great War also had a drastic effect on that feature, the wide thematic range of Delarue-Mardrus' early contributions being replaced by an intense and grimly naturalistic concentration on the war and its aftermath. When "Le Secret d'Amanit" was published that range was only just beginning to broaden out again, and *Amanit* is unusual among her longer stories in featuring a fantastic motif, albeit much more discreetly and ambiguously than her early works.

One of the most remarkable features of the fictional world contained in Delarue-Mardrus' early short stories is the role played therein by amour and marriage. Whereas most fiction by female writers of the period routinely featured characters whose primary obsession is amorous, taking it for granted that amour provides the most powerful incentives and the most precious possible rewards in adult life, Delarue-Mardrus' early fiction almost makes a fetish out of the irrelevance of amour to many of her characters, and the minority who fall victim to infatuation in her stories are not merely disappointed, but devastated in consequence. In her early prose works, "true love" is a disaster best avoided, marriage and adultery being incidents of scant importance to those who can indulge in them harmlessly. That attitude shifted considerably when she began to produce longer stories of a relentlessly naturalistic character, which were forced by the necessities of conventional realism to bring amour into much more frequent and sharper focus as a desire and ambition, although her subtexts retained a jaundiced and cynical attitude to it. *Amanit* is not only exceptional in restoring an element of fantasy to its plot but also—and perhaps more importantly, in the context of the author's work—in making a determined attempt to describe and analyze a successful amorous relationship.

The fictitious amour in *Amanit* is heterosexual, as are the amours featured in the great majority—but not all—of the author's works. Perhaps it is unsurprising that she found the idea of successful heterosexual amour very difficult to imagine, and it is certainly unsurprising that she thought alternatives difficult to mention, let alone to analyze, in fiction aimed at a mass audience. Several male authors of the period, including Catulle Mendès and Pierre Louÿs, had made extravagant use of lesbian lust in their works, but in a salacious manner intended to titillate male voyeurism—a strategy more likely to offend misandric female writers than to appeal to them. By eliminating any mention of the possibility from the great majority of her works, however, Delarue-Mardrus was presumably not unaware of a certain intrinsic hypocrisy in the works in question, and that awareness is not irrelevant to the peculiarities of *Amanit*—or, for that matter, to the two shorter stories—but it is an understandable decision on her part.

The sum of these factors ensured that *Amanit* would be one of the most distinctive works penned by a highly distinctive writer. It is even less coherently-organized than the invariably-patchy story-series she wrote for *Le Journal*, but that does not detract from the interest of its theme, and the kind of narrative fragmentation that it employs produces a quasi-kaleidoscopic effect that is not uninteresting in itself as an artistic endeavor. The novella is certainly an unusual and original work, and also thought-provoking in its tacit and explicit challenges to literary convention. Its translation is an intriguing addendum to the often-brilliant stories featured in *The Last Siren and Other Stories*.

✳

The translation of *Amanit* was made from a copy of the 1929 Fasquelle edition. The translations of "Le Secret d'Amanit" and "La Momie consolatrice" were made from the copies of the relevant issues of *Le Journal* reproduced on the Bibliothèque Nationale's *gallica* website.

—Brian Stableford

EARLY STORIES

THE CONSOLATORY MUMMY

DECIDEDLY, the princess would not return to France. Her sulky voyage away from Paris, undertaken in a moment of moral disgust, would be prolonged indefinitely.

Christmas came, followed by the first of January. Those Christian and Occidental festivals illuminated the hotels of Cairo, agitating the Europeans accumulated in the foreign capital, and while the midnight feasts and balls filled the city with noise, while the German and American waltzes spun around Christmas trees and under the beribboned mistletoe, crouching not far away in the night, perfectly forgotten by humans, was the Sphinx, who knows everything, and before whom—among other corteges—the poor Jewish family to whom we owe our God doubtless once filed.

On the night of the twenty-fifth of December, in the shadow of the stone beast, a patient donkey-drover was wandering, waiting for a client who did not arrive. He was holding his evangelical donkey by the bridle, and, with his mantle over his head, reproduced exactly, in the finishing moonlight, the silhouette of Saint Joseph. Perhaps the Virgin and her child Jesus were asleep in that hole in the sand, represented by a Bedouin women clutching her tiny baby Bedouin, both enveloped in the same veil; but no one, among those making merry in Cairo, was thinking of making the true pilgrimage of memory, the nocturnal and silent pilgrimage toward the desert sands, toward the Sphinx, as eternal as a rock, whose human eyes had seen the people of the Old Testament and the New Testament pass by.

In any case, great Arab festivals, Muslim commemorations and the return of pilgrims departed for Mecca, coincided with the Christian joys, with the result that Cairo was no longer anything but a rumor of pleasure for a fortnight. And that was fitting for that city of fine weather, a capital without nervousness, a warm cauldron in which races were simmering.

It was very sensible that, in spite of the profound hostilities that rub shoulders daily under the sky of Egypt, and in spite of the tendency of contemporary Egyptians toward seething ideas, nothing would ever burst forth in the center, forever pacified by the fatal sun. The wisdom of the Orient is perhaps in its nonchalance; and cannot see in what respect European restlessness, which is always turning, in sum, around a question mark, is superior to Oriental repose. The Occidental interrogates the unknown feverishly, while the Oriental slumbers. Which of the two is the more reasonable, given that silence is the sole response?

Then again, everything is a matter of climate. The same sunlight that gives birth to palm trees and banana trees naturally engenders nonchalance and indifference, just as our rainy countries bring to light poplars and ash trees. After all, it is a matter of living. When death comes to take one and the other, nothing tells us that the true Oriental, the man who does not rack his brain thinking differently from his race, has not lived better than us.

Patricia did not bother analyzing these things, good for the minds of artists and writers. It was not that she was incapable of following an idea, but she did not like to think about herself or that which gave her pleasure. For some time, she had found that pleasure, without exactly knowing why, in frequenting the eminently indigenous quarters as much as possible. That was because, in those places, her sense of harmony found itself fully satisfied.

Among the houses that were crumbling like the past, as seductive as the past and as neglected as the past, the red houses with mashrabiyas of brown wood, among the winding back-streets above which one could only see a thin strip of blue sky, she watched the typical passers-by: true Orientals with beautiful garments, the men and women of the people who wander, intoxicated by idleness, along the little shops of the souks, dragging their lemon yellow slippers and their black mantles in the millenary dust and never seem to be in haste. The swarm of popular Cairo, colors, perfumes and noises, the colors of black women with gilded noses, men in robes of all colors, perfumes of incense as at mass, peremptory odors of heaped-up spices, gusts of jasmine, amber and rose, come from who knows where; the sounds of voices and wheels, disputes and laughter, the rhymed refrains of ambulant merchants of fruits or sweet beverages, a numerous and singing rumor dominated by the petty dry music made on the beaten earth by the hooves of white donkeys, mingled with the clicking of their blue collars and their sequins: all of that was what the princess loved, all that she would regret when she quit Egypt.

✹

However, as February approached, a few gray clouds arrived, with a little rain, and the temperature dropped again. That was a scandal in the world of the hotels. Because the thermometer marked ten above zero at night in January, the Europeans found Egypt dishonest.

Princesse Patricia shut herself away in her Savoy again, resuming her corner near the fireplace. Lying in ambush behind her lorgnette, she watched the comings and goings of her sisters, the pretty women of all countries. She also saw the autochthonous women coming in and going out, the beautiful ladies of Cairo, with their Biblical profiles under modern hats and their splendid eyes, the last daughters of Rachel and Leah, as magnificent as paintings by Delacroix in spite of the tight and barbaric dresses imposed by fashion.

An atmosphere of perfect modern elegance replaced, for the princess, the sparkle of the old streets, temporarily drowned by rain and mud. She also liked to study slyly the Kronzprinzessin,[1] whom all eyes devoured and who, always sitting in the same corner among her ladies in waiting, smoked Salonika cigarettes, the gilded butts

1 Cecilie von Mecklenburg-Schwerin (1886-1954), the wife of the German Crown Prince Wilhelm, son of Emperor Wilhelm II, an important fashion icon of the pre-war period.

of which American billionaires picked up for their collections. Patricia loved watching her, not because she would be the Empress of Germany some day but because she was charming, with her child-like laugh, her bright teeth, her fresh cheeks, her easily-amused eyes, and her little child's nose, corrected by two perfectly-designed eyebrows, imperious and precise, which mingled all the necessary royalty in the face of the pretty little woman.

How young she is! Patricia thought. And immediately: *I'm even younger* . . .

She preferred not to repeat herself until she had passed forty, but she told herself that if her soul ever appeared in her features, the face would be seen of the most definitively disappointed woman . . .

"Madame Mortin?" she commenced, for she suddenly had need of compliments. And the lady companion, in a bleak and amiable voice, obliged.

Oh, how irritating you are, thought the princess, then. And quickly, she sent the lady away on some fallacious mission—letters to copy or information to look up in books,

One day, when it was raining, she went to the museum of Egyptian antiquities. She had already visited that museum several times, but always in the company of messieurs or ladies full of science, who had spoiled it with explanations.

That afternoon, even Madame Mortin was eliminated. The princess wanted to be alone. She had woken up too somber to tolerate any presence by her side.

When she found herself facing those she sought, she gazed at the mummies for a long time, without even thinking about taking out her lorgnette. There was no one in the museum except, in each hall, one of those indigenous guardians who seem to have emerged from the display-cases themselves, where they had been enclosed and embalmed in abolished ages.

They were there, the ladies of the past, the priestesses and the queens, wrapped in beautiful colors, all new, as smooth as fish, lying in their boxes of painted wood with their eyes with golden eyelids, staring through the glass Those dead sirens had been asleep, lying in the respectful sand, until the day when, gilded finds, they had been surprised and disinterred in order to be offered, like captives, to the miscreant gaze of our century.

To live in that epoch . . . Patricia repeated to herself.

Visions passed before her contemplative gaze. She let herself go to the dreams we form in the presence of things of old, and which are not, in fact, merely dreams; for the mummies, when they were alive, lived in accordance with their personal modernity; and the fabulous did not exist five thousand years ago any more than it exists today among us. The Egyptians of the Pharaonic dynasties were probably very preoccupied by being of their time, of being contemporaries. They certainly did not know that one day, their epoch would appear to the eyes of dreamers as an enchanted time. They had fanaticism, pride, cupidity, intelligence and all the motive forces that lead us. Perhaps they were our superiors, but they were not marvelous, in the sense that we mean it when we look at the sarcophagi. And doubtless our present civilization, which seems to us to be denuded of all prestige, will make future generations dream, even more than we dream before the likes of Ramses and Amenophis.

As she was roaming at random, going toward whatever tempted her gaze, always drawn to bodies still wrapped, which seemed the chrysalides of death, she perceived in a little corner of a small room a form that was dissimulated in the shadow, the form of a millenary woman, stark naked, having no other vestment than the debris of large necklaces around her neck: turquoises, as dead as their owner, which seemed to have strangled the dead woman. Residues of hair, a precise face with revulsed eyeballs, a pinched nose, a mouth wide open over two rows of bright teeth, with a dry tongue emerging to one side, frightful and bitter: Lady Amanit, priestess of Hathor.

The princess was absolutely alone in the hall. She sat down on her heels in order to look at the priestess more closely. Such a convulsion twisted that little cadaver of a woman that one might have thought that she had scarcely ceased agonizing.

How she suffered! thought the princess.

Her large blue and green eyes itemized untiringly.

And that body moved, and those eyes gazed, and those cheeks quivered, and that hair was warmed, and those nostrils respired, and those terrible, beautiful teeth smiled, and that tongue, that dry tongue, spoke! And now, all of that, which composed a woman, is nothing more than that doll of elongated wood behind glass, which no one can remark because it has been set aside. Lady Amanit? What did she think, Lady Amanit? How did she live? What was there in her empty head? In spite of those three or four thousand years, one can see how beautiful she once was!

Instinctively, the princess passed her ungloved hand over her own face, feeling her own warm cheek and the form of her teeth behind her warm cheek. And now confused thoughts were born in her living head, in the depths of her frivolous and melancholy brain, facing the dead head of Lady Amanit.

I lament growing old, she repeated, *I lament growing old* . . .

Under the intense gaze of the princess, Lady Amanit, horrible and charming, did not get up from her eternity. But we know nothing of the mystery of death. Perhaps the woman's gaze, fixed ardently on the mummy, endowed that narrow hollow and dry body, and the deserted skull, momentarily, with a sort of borrowed soul. At any rate, Patricia sensed that an unforgettable counsel, a supreme consolation, came to her from the depths of shadow where the priestess of Hathor dwelt, immobile and convulsed, suffering forever in a mute scream.

"Yes, look at me well, and then feel your forehead and your ribs, in order to assure yourself that your heart and your brain are still there. And be glad even of growing old, because growing old is living. And be glad still to possess everything necessary to think, love and suffer. Perhaps you came to Egypt in order to learn from a mummy the pleasure of living: the pleasure, in spite of everything, of living. What do epochs and civilizations matter? The only thing that counts is breathing, gazing, hearing, moving and touching, even if nothing results from all that but sighs and sobs. Oh, if only I could still sob, I who am no longer anything more than a dusty object in the depths of this shadow! Look at my teeth! They alone have remained identical to what they were. But for thousands of years they have no longer bitten anything but emptiness and silence. If only that glass did not separate us, you could touch them with your fingertip; they are my eternal youth. And merely touching them might perhaps render me a second of life . . . oh, to live! Was it necessary for this body to respire for thirty or forty years and that it should then lie in immobility for four thousand years? You who lament growing old, what is old age compared with annihilation?"

The daylight was beginning to diminish in the empty halls. Lightly, Patricia stood up, in a rustle of intimate silk. She could not reach the face of her sister, the dead woman, but before going away, she blew her a kiss of passionate gratitude from her fingertips.

AMANIT'S SECRET

A T the moment when so many diverse emotions are being directed toward the violated tomb of Tutankhamen,[1] this is what I remember.

The open sarcophagus revealed Amanit to us, or rather her form, for she still retained, in spite of being blackened and fissured, her funereal sheath, a kind of painted cardboard that sometimes, after thousands of years in the sepulcher, reappears to the curious eyes of Egyptologists in a new state, in truth: fresh colors, intact gold, immaculate substance.

Amanit, the two or three competent persons present had told us, was a princess of the royal family, the daughter of kings, whom death had surprised in the flower of her age, when she was not yet married.

The sheath having been removed, while the unwrapping commenced, as the only woman admitted to the audience to see the princess resuscitated, I darted a gaze over the precious cadaver that was certainly more impressed

1 The discovery of the tomb of Tutankhamen in 1922 by Howard Carter was one of the biggest news stories of that year and sparked a dramatic renewal of interest in Egyptology.

than those of the other spectators, because it was, on the one hand, the first time that it had been given to me to witness such an exhumation, while the messieurs present had become habituated to ceremonies of that sort over the years; and on the other hand, a fellow feeling, if you will, linked me with that feminine being who, for me, was not merely a document—a page of history, an archeological curiosity—but also a kind of sister of old, a creature of my species, whose remains, fallen into sacrilegious hands, had contained all the mysteries of our sex.

Shall I confess, in brief, that I was almost embarrassed to see that young foreign woman—foreign by virtue of her race and epoch, but still a young woman by virtue of her conservation and her form, and whose name and rank were known to us—undressed by men?

"Amanit," I said to myself, "you were pharaonic, and merely by virtue of that millenary term, we believe ourselves authorized to violate your eternity. You were pharaonic, and therefore, for our modern mind, *fabulous*. The long death in which you have reposed for centuries has made you something other than human, almost a statue, a sort of idol whose flesh and bone no longer have any fraternity with our flesh and bone. Embalming has changed you into gold. The slightest contemporary death would provoke in us a frisson of horror far more sensible than the cold curiosity with which we are leaning over you at present.

"And yet, Lady Amanit, young woman who died prematurely, long before Jesus Christ, personally, I cannot help imagining you as you were in the time when your desiccated breast was breathing. Similar to many other adolescents in this land of Egypt where nothing changes, like the Muslims encountered everywhere here in Cairo, and who continue, at this very moment, to circulate in the museum in which we are gathered, you had large dark eyes—probably afflicted, without it being too obvious, by the endemic ophthalmia of the region—a smooth, dark complexion, beautiful bright teeth, a little nose with nostrils opening and closing alternately, a long and slender silhouette, delicate wrists and ankles, hands and feet already mummified by the harsh sunlight; and your little sphinx-like head contained the thoughts of your age, which are very nearly the same in all epochs and all latitudes, for youth is monotonous and easily decipherable: coquetry, naïve vanity, ingenuous ambition, and probably, surely, amours . . .

"Amour! Were your dreams dedicated to the son of the Pharaoh to whom you were destined by protocol, or had your heart chosen of its own accord the object of its emotions? Who was the young fellow who made your large eyes dream, and the sight of whom activated the movements of your little thorax, still intact, where a heart like ours beat then? It is not the secret of the hermetic Egypt that I am evoking presently; it is your secret, that of a woman extracted from the peaceful darkness, yours, that of an orphan of your time, prey to barbaric contemporaries, devoid of pity for your deranged eternity . . ."

Coincidence? Telepathy? Supernatural? Everyone else's exclamations covered mine. I had just turned my head in order not to look at the vulgar scene of the amphitheater, the scientist's scalpel attacking without hesitation the sacred body of the mummy.

An imperceptible movement of recoil was manifest in our little group.

In fact: "Oh look!" exclaimed the operator. "It's the first time I've seen that! The mummy is pregnant!"

An entire agitation followed those words. A romance surged forth from the hieroglyphic bier: a mummy of the first class, a daughter of royal blood, dead before marriage . . .

"We have it! We have it!" cried the scientist. "Oh, look at this . . . !"

All necks were craning, all eyes following the trajectory that he was designing with his finger, the trajectory of the long crack that split the little desiccated head alongside the temple.

"Murdered!" concluded the scientist. "Lady Amanit wasn't married. The child that she was carrying without saying so was the result of a crime inadmissible in her father's palace, the fruit of a forbidden amour for some inferior, who could not become the husband of a royal princess. The violent death of the young woman was surely passed off as an accident; the daughter of a king could not be dishonored."

I saw young Amanit again later, in her painted coffin, which had been covered by a glass case: young Amanit, having become a museum object like so many others of her race. But beside her, a tiny skeleton reposed, that of her natural child, the child of amour, which a twentieth-century doctor had delivered, finally revealing her secret, after more than ten thousand years of clandestine pregnancy.

AMANIT

PROLOGUE

CHARLES-ÉTIENNE, the only son of Jean Masserand, had just announced to all and sundry his engagement to Geneviève Le Rieux. That was not astonishing, for the two young people had loved one another since childhood. The hubbub of the soirée increased amid the outmoded furniture of the apartment in which the Academician had been living for twenty years, where his wife had died and his son had grown up, a studious adolescent scarcely knowing that he was handsome. The guests, in three rooms that were too small, and overheated by slow-burning stoves, were talking about the engagement.

The door opened for a tall young woman. She did not pose her almond-shaped eyes on anyone. Like black and white enamel, they had a gaze that could not fail to cause a frisson. At first one saw nothing but them, an indecipherable enigma. In a pale olive complexion, delicately balanced features, a short nose, a thick and crimson mouth, all without any make-up, was surrounded by natural curls that were too long to be fashionable, with blue reflections near the temples. That museum head, on a flexible neck, was supported by a body slender at the hips and broad at the shoulders, which, beneath the divine golden dress, ought to have been a smooth, brown and slippery eel.

She passed through, seeking her host. Behind her, there was a unique murmur:

"Who is she . . . ? Who is she?"

At the back of the room, Jean Masserand, surrounded by a circle of admirers intent on making him shine in spite of his customary charming modesty, blinked his blue eyes upon the apparition heading toward him.

"Oh! Princess Antinides!" he exclaimed, his hands extended.

"Master . . ." she said.

The guests looked on.

"Where's Charles-Étienne? It's necessary that I introduce you to him right away!"

She smiled. Her teeth glinted. The whispers around her fell silent. There was silence again, striking after the noise of the soirée. One might have thought that everyone was waiting for an explanation. There was no movement, except that the old Duc de Chables could have been remarked letting himself fall into an armchair.

"Finally, here you are, Charlet! If you knew everything that the princess told me about Egypt the other day, at Taillefer's. I truly didn't believe, Madame, that you'd have the goodness to come this evening. I told you, didn't I, that my son is an Egyptologist? I was thinking about him all the time when you were talking about Elephantine, that palace . . . he hasn't yet been to Egypt, you know, any more than I have."

Charles-Étienne bowed. It was noted that he blushed in a manner that was more fearful than charmed. That was the general impression, in fact; Princess Antinides, so abnormally beautiful, had something about her that sowed fear.

The eyes of black and white enamel, immobilized and dangerous, considered Charles-Étienne, the wave of his hair, chestnut in the thickness and blond at the surface, as if gilded by the sun, his blue irises, so fresh between two curtains of blond lashes, the pure and masculine design of his clean-shaven face, and the beautiful line of his youthful body, intimidated by her.

"Geneviève?" he appealed—and, almost in a whisper: "My fiancée . . ."

Geneviève Le Rieux gave her hand to be shaken with the slightly gauche stiffness that added to her personality. Coiffed by pale braids, her thin lips and her great gray gaze were icy; her silhouette was that of a Gothic virgin.

"A sandwich?" she asked, politely and coldly. "A glass of orangeade?"

A moment later, the petrifaction of the drawing rooms gave way. Social convention regained the upper hand. The reformed groups rediscovered speech. Charles-Étienne and the princess, sitting apart, were chatting, observed from a distance. The Academician was trying to hold off his flatterers, who had drawn near again. Feminine laughter burst out and an argument commenced in the direction of the study.

It was not yet midnight. The reception was approaching its peak.

The old Duc de Chables, as pale as death between his white side-whiskers, found the means to approach Jean Masserand and touched his shoulder. Seeing his confidential manner, the admirers recoiled slightly. It was said that Chables was nearly ninety years old. A slightly mocking admiration surrounded his astonishing conservation.

"Who is that woman?" he asked, his voice hoarse.

"It's Princess Antinides, of Alexandria, Greek by extraction. I made her acquaintance at the home of my colleague Taillefer last week. She knows heaps of things about Egypt that will interest my son. Impressive, isn't she?"

Old Chables' hand trembled on his friend's sleeve.

"That woman," he choked, "resembles, feature for feature, the misfortune of my life!"

"Bah!" said the Academician, turning round, almost laughing. But he shivered before the duc's face.

"I'd like to talk to her, Masserand. Will you introduce me?"

"Gladly, dear friend."

Stiffly, the old man kissed the strange little hand, as dry and dark as a mummy's. Charles-Étienne withdrew, searching with his eyes for his fiancée.

"You'll excuse my indiscretion, Madame," the duc commenced, sitting down in the young man's place, "but are you not the granddaughter or great-granddaughter of the beautiful Belkis Hanoum Effendi of Constantinople?"

The magnificent teeth glinted again. Without the slightest accent, the princess replied in contralto: "Oh, not at all, Monsieur! I'm Greek; Belkis is a Turkish name, and I don't have a drop of Turkish blood in my veins."

"Pardon me again. You're absolutely sure of your genealogy? It's just that . . ."

The Duc de Chables did not say another word. A unanimous exclamation filled the series of three buzzing rooms. Having stood up abruptly without a cry, stiff and funereal, the old man fell backwards, fainted or dead.

I

LIKE an imperishable magic wand, childhood—even that of the twentieth century—retains the charming power to create marvels.

Do you have the time to observe children? Divine the heartbeat of that little girl carrying something from the end of the garden in her apron, merely by her face and the fashion in which she is advancing. What treasure is she hiding? Three varnished chestnuts, or a large flint with a shiny hollow, or a quivering naked frog. With that, enchantment is created for several hours.

What is that little boy, who does not seem to be thinking about anything, contemplating in that corner of the attic? The invisible thing that he will only forget in death—for the memories of childhood, the secret realm of all humans, contain an intimate enchantment that one must never try to recount to others, made of dreams much more than realities.

A former farmhouse converted into a holiday home had to contain, for the seven individuals who resided therein, the best part of the existence of the Masserand family.

In that epoch, the Masserand grandparents were still alive, as was the fragile Madame Jean Masserand, the ideal mother of a little boy as blond as her, and the poetic spouse of an unknown young writer.

In that farmhouse full of joy, Jean Masserand found his literary destiny, and abandoned poorly inspired novels in order to devote himself to the history that would subsequently enable him to enter the Académie. That came from an old library rich in forgotten documents that was part of the house rented to traveling friends. And while his father discovered his future thus, little Charles-Étienne also encountered his: the unique love of his life, Geneviève.

At the Château de Bellecour, which gave its name to the village, a little seigneurie buried in a series of profound parks, the last two Messieurs de Bellecour—one of whom was a childless widower and the other a bachelor—were bringing up their grandniece Geneviève, with the aid of a gray-haired housekeeper. She was the daughter of their cherished niece, who had died bringing that unhealthy doll into the world. The young husband had killed himself in despair.

In the depths of the silent château, with her two great-uncles, who were passionate about hunting, and their aged housekeeper, the tragic child might never have met Charles-Étienne Masserand, a Parisian gamin who surged forth in the landscape one fine summer evening. On the first Sunday following the installation in the Beautilleul farm, however, at the village high mass, to which his mother and grandmother took him, Charles-Étienne, bored by the Roman ceremony, raised his eyes just as the harmonium commenced an admirable Bach prelude. An old retired priest, an obscure and profoundly erudite musician, came to Bellecour to play every Sunday, and doubtless played much more for himself than for the peasants who listened to him.

Charles-Étienne was only eight years old. He was nevertheless subject to the august frisson of that music. Until then, the bellowing of the cantors had drowned out everything.

The urchin saw, in the thirteenth-century stained-glass window, the pride of the little church, a Sainte Radegonde of painted glass and light offering to God the Father, between two excessively long hands, her monastery of Sainte-Croix de Poitiers, a miniature abbey more precious than a reliquary; he saw the golden tresses of the canonized queen, her translucent green and red robe girdled with lead, the décor of three colors that surrounded her; and that royal phantom, momentarily associated with the Bach prelude, created in the soul of the child a plenitude of harmony to which he could only submit, without analyzing it. He was only eight years old.

Oppressed by the disproportionate lyricism that invaded his little heart, he wanted to turn his gaze away from the haunted window. Below the window, however, in the shadow of the bench of honor, there was—a third frisson—another queen of France, this one very thin and wholly alive: a beautiful demoiselle seven years old, carrying her missal exactly as the first was caring her abbey, her face between two similar golden tresses, under a velvet bonnet that copied the saint's hood: an identical profile, and identical attitude, a little Radegonde of flesh and bone, at least as pale as the big one, and, like her, the very incarnation of the short passage of Bach.

There are moments of which the thunderbolt can never be communicated to anyone else, even when adulthood, arrived much later, finally permits their expression. Charles-Étienne did not know, at that precise moment, that he was receiving, like a strange sacrament, the illumination of his entire life; however, seized by a kind of shock, he squeezed his frightened mother's hand violently. And it was from that moment on that he loved Geneviève with an amour so elevated and so powerful that nothing could any longer detach him from her.

There was a tiresome childish refrain that fatigued the Beautilleul farm for a fortnight: "I want to see the little girl from the church. I want you to invite her, or her to invite me."

It was necessary to wait for two Sundays before, on the emergence from high mass, the curé, who had come to see his new parishioners, judged it appropriate to introduce the inhabitants of the château and those of the former farm to one another. The Messieurs de Bellecour and the housekeeper thought that the Mesdames Masserand seemed pleasant. The children looked one another in the eyes, little Charles-Étienne blushing and trembling, little Geneviève glacial and self-controlled.

"They're almost the same age," said the elder Bellecour. "One of these days you must bring us your boy. They can play together."

II

THEY played together.

The parks of Bellecour had umbels taller than the two children. Immobilized on the edge of the largest lawn, they continued on the first day that Charles-Étienne was invited, to look one another in the eyes. The housekeeper, sitting a short distance away, was sewing silently. Geneviève, a very precious person, was always guarded, even at play time. She seemed slightly discomfited by the presence of young Masserand. Having never frequented other children, her obscure instinct was doubtless revolted by the intruder. Her gray eyes did not smile. Silently, she seemed to be waiting for him to go away.

Charles-Étienne's heart was beating rapidly. He felt that he was in an atmosphere of prodigy. While repeating his refrain he had not believed that his wish might ever be granted. He asked for the little girl from the church as he might have asked for the moon. She had been revealed to him in the manner of a phantasm issued from the harmonium that had started to play at that moment. A harmonium, at mass, plays alone at a certain moment, as the bells sound alone through the countryside when the hour of the Angelus arrives. Does one ever think about the bell-ringers? When Bach had been manifest, that Sunday, could he have come from a dusty old priest sitting in the stall next to the nave? Like the stained-glass window and like Geneviève herself, all of that had been part of the realms of dreams. And now, Geneviève was there, on the edge of the grass, shaded by foliage, under an immense blue sky traversed by white clouds, and Charles-Étienne could only gaze at her without speaking.

"Well, aren't you going to play?" shouted the housekeeper, from a distance.

The session of hypnotism ended with those words, a heavy reality launched like a brutal stone into the phantasmagoria.

Geneviève must have been habituated to obedience. "It's necessary to play!" said her shrill voice.

But she was still not smiling. She turned round, seemingly searching for something to do, and suddenly picked two daisies forgotten by nature in the August grass.

Charles-Étienne, remaining where he was, watched the two daisies shifting in the excessively long fingers of the miniature Sainte Radegonde.

"There!" said the little girl, finally.

At a distance, she presented the most extraordinary little thing. Between her fingers there were no longer two corollas but a single stem with a daisy at each end. It is a trick that certain children know; but Charles-Étienne was seeing it for the first time. Meanwhile, he dared not pronounce a syllable, or budge a step.

"That doesn't amuse you?" she said, scornfully. She pirouetted, threw away the flower and started to run.

Then a flood of heroism tore poor Charlet's breast. He had a desire to do something unexpected in order to conquer the creature with the cold eyes who only had to touch flowers to work miracles. He bounded forward in order to overtake her. Why did he not know how to walk on his hands and turn cartwheels?

Beside himself, his arms raised toward the clouds, he ran along the pathways. In order to manifest his joy, he felt capable of flying. Then, stupidly, he let himself fall to the ground and he rolled in the grass with ridiculous gesticulations.

Geneviève stopped and looked at him. She only knew grown-ups; an invalid herself, she had almost nothing child-like about her. Suddenly, she started laughing until tears came, the trill of a blackbird that made the astonished housekeeper shudder in the distance.

She was laughing! Charles-Étienne had a desire to cry. Such a success threw him into a kind of crisis. He exaggerated his antics. Lying on his back, he kicked his legs in the air, got up and fell down again. On all fours he started to bite the lawn, and, his mouth full of grass, crimson, his blond hair in the wind, he stood up again to look at Geneviève under his nose. She had never seen such a spectacle. A little scandal and a great deal of admiration cut off her breath. Were little boys like that?

From the depths of feminine darkness the sentiment rose within her that he was only throwing himself about so wildly to please her. She sensed the strength, the good health and the zeal of the little man, all put at the service of her frailty of a delicate child. She sensed, at the same time, the power of her own weakness. Ceasing to look at him, she turned her back and walked away, dignified and upright.

Henceforth, she incessantly welcomed the advances of her little comrade with the same appearance of not admitting them.

Distant in appearance but fundamentally charmed, she received him when he came without even saying bonjour, and she never embraced him. Only once was she taken to the Beautilleul farm for the afternoon, and she was ill the next day, having eaten too many forbidden things. It was decided thereafter that young Masserand would only come to see her.

He preferred that convention. The somber parks and the outdated château impressed him. Out of his element, his emotion was even greater. The perpetual presence of the housekeeper, which made every game somewhat stilted, added to everything else to enclose Geneviève in a kind of enchanted circle.

Without losing anything of the past, the eight-year-old boy reinvented chivalry. The lady sometimes consented to descend from her tower, but the exploits of her knight left her indifferent. In that company, she gave the impression of lowering herself.

Guided by her impulses, however, she had seemingly-inspired moments that compensated for all her disdain.

"Come here, Charlet! Stand very close to me. Look at my finger in the air. Do you see my beautiful ring?"

It was the crescent of the new moon in the crepuscular sky.

Returning home alone in the old armoried caleche of the Messieurs de Bellecour, the little poet continued his dream.

Simultaneously admitted and rejected, his heart full of happiness and humiliation, he counted on his fingers the days that separated him from his next visit to the château.

Furthermore, his parents knew nothing of his secret. Apart from the fact that parents are routinely the last to be informed of their children's secrets, how could Charles-Étienne have told them his? He did not even know that he had a secret.

His father and mother said to one another: "Charlet likes going to Bellecour and the two old country squires seem to be glad that he goes. So much the better!"

When they came out of mass on Sunday they decided the next rendezvous. Sometimes, young Masserand had the dolor of not seeing Geneviève. "She was suffering yesterday," said the great-uncles, sadly. "She has to stay in her room." And in Charlet's heart the ingenuous idyll was intensified by the fact of those illnesses, too frequently repeated. It was another manner that Geneviève had of being inaccessible.

The only time that she allowed herself to be persuaded to play at running, the housekeeper was seen to hurry forward after a few minutes.

"It's necessary not to run like that! It's bad for her! Can't you see how hot she is?"

And because she was hot, amazingly, it was necessary to wrap her in a shawl.

Complication, mystery and muted threats of death prowled around that magical little girl . . .

The departure of the Masserand family at the end of the season was a tragedy for the unfortunate Charlet.

To his passionate adieux, Geneviève responded with an enigmatic silence and a polar gaze, having been unable, even at the moment of quitting him, to decide to embrace him.

Would she regret her summer companion a little? How could he know? She seemed rather to be relieved by his long absence.

He tried writing to her, and received no response. Meanwhile, a few words she had said to him one day had to sustain him and orientate the days that it was necessary to pass far from her.

"If I were a boy and I went to school, I'd like to be the first in the class, and to come home for the vacations with the prize of honor."

A mediocre student until then, Charles-Étienne surprised his masters and his parents the following winter by the notes he never ceased to obtain. How long that school year seemed, at the end of which shone, almost as distant as the afterlife, the paradise of the long vacation!

It was furnished with his prize of honor that the gamin returned to Beautilleul. It was solely in order to present it to her, at the moment of their first encounter, that he had worked so hard.

Perhaps she'll embrace me?

But she did not embrace him. Taller and diaphanous between her long and brilliant blonde braids, she only murmured: "You must be proud." That was all—but it was a great deal, even so. He felt recompensed. Impetuously, he promised in secret to redouble his efforts in the next term. In that little masculine soul, ambition was born.

He dared not make the reproaches he had prepared on the subject of his unanswered letters. He never dared anything under the gaze that chilled him and burned him.

III

THE beautiful afternoons among the shady trees and the bright lawns recommenced, under the surveillance of the housekeeper. No progress in the amity of little Le Rieux. Many a time, without even seeking a pretext, she deserted her suitor in the middle of a game that she seemed to be enjoying, or at the most exciting part of the prize of honor that they were reading together: *The History of Ancient Egypt*. She returned to the château alone, leaving him to finish the day with the housekeeper.

I bore her, he thought, with tears in his eyes. *She's even less kind to me than last year.*

And without chagrin, simply in order no longer to be importunate, the nine-year-old child, humble and self-sacrificing, plunged into the meditations of a man, and envisaged heroically the possibility of never returning to Bellecour again.

Then, like a broken career, his scholarly future appeared bleak, and henceforth devoid of any desire to obtain good notes or any prize whatsoever.

No one at home suspected such a drama in the heart of such a young child. His father, too mild, and his mother, too suave, and his grandparents, ever intent on spoiling him, never knew that, bewitched by the empire of a sick and haughty little girl, their handsome Charlet, white and pink, so healthy beneath his baby-blond hair, with his floral eyes, had drunk at the age of eight the philter of an Yseult no taller than him.

The vacation was about to terminate again. A despair above his age commenced in the soul of Charles-Étienne. He told himself that the next season would put an end to his camaraderie with Geneviève. Even more distant, she would end up simply refusing to admit him into her life.

Strictly brought up by the housekeeper, she knew that she was the queen of the château of which she was the soul and the reason for existence. A vacillating flame, jealously protected, the last vestige of a dying family, her will of a little invalid would always be obeyed, even though she was apparently so docile to the instruction and orders of the ever-present chaperone.

That's it . . . decidedly, I no longer please her . . .

A ridiculous rag doll, which she had fabricated with the aid of the housekeeper and painted like a clown, was the basis of the games on the big lawn.

The manner in which Charlet played with the doll had revolted Geneviève at first, but subsequently, she became passionate for such a great novelty.

The poor puppet simply served as a ball. The two children threw the doll to one another, laughing to see it fluttering in the air. After that came the rackets, of which it was the shuttlecock. Finally, Geneviève invented the game of throwing it into the branches of the big fir tree in order to see it caught by its grotesque skirt in desperate attitudes. Armed with an apple-pole, Charlet had then to unhook it, amid difficulties that made all the pleasure of the game. Geneviève, sitting a few paces away in the grass, watched him fencing, criticizing all of his gestures.

How he would have liked to shine by means of his skill! But the pole was much too large and much too heavy for his strength, and every time he missed his thrust the ironic little chimera uttered cries of joy.

One afternoon, the doll was thrown so high that the pole could not reach it.

"That's it," Charlet concluded, after many futile attempts. "It's going to stay there forever now."

At those words, Geneviève bounded to her feet.

"I don't want that," she said, her teeth clenched. "I need it, you hear?"

She had gone even paler than usual.

At an order so peremptory, and an anguish so violent expressed on her little face, Charlet did not hesitate. He was finally about to be the hero of a fine adventure, before the gray eyes that devoured him.

"Have no fear!" he declared. "I'll climb up and get it."

What were the children doing over there? The housekeeper squinted in their direction. She perceived Geneviève, her nose in the air, under the fir tree. *Ah! always the doll and the pole. That's all right.* And the old woman resumed her tranquil needlework.

Charlet climbed up to the first branches easily, but the difficulties commenced there. Vertigo was about to grip him. Once he was sitting astride a branch in the crown of the fir tree, he realized that going to fetch the doll from where it was represented an almost impossible enterprise.

"Go on, then!" shouted the mocking voice of Geneviève from down below.

He dared not respond that he was afraid. His honor was engaged. *Too bad!* he said to himself. He extended his arm to catch the branch he needed and to hoist himself on to it if he could. His fingers reached the rough bark, and were skinned by clinging on to it. With a single thrust, his legs let go. Suspended over the void momentarily, with a noise of little branches breaking, with a cry of fear and pain, he fell at Geneviève's feet.

The eyes that he raised to her were full of agonized tears. The unfortunate child had just broken his leg.

The little girl did not utter an exclamation. She leaned over her victim phlegmatically.

"You're going to die . . ." she murmured. She turned toward the housekeeper. "Come quickly, Madame Leroy! Charlet has fallen!"

Calmly, she knelt down next to the injured boy and palpated him gently. He groaned.

"It's there!" she said, in the tone of a surgeon.

The housekeeper came running, upset. "Oh my God! Oh my God!"

The old woman continued to exclaim while turning round and round. Geneviève cut into her emotion.

"Take him in your arms, Madame Leroy. It's necessary to carry him to the house; and have the carriage harnessed. We'll lie him down while waiting to be able to take him home. The carriage can pass through the town to pick up the doctor."

The tranquility of that little authoritarian voice dominated the situation. The dramatic cortege made its entrance to the château amid the panic of the servants. Messieurs de Bellecour were not there.

When the invalid was stretched out in the caleche in the arms of Madame Leroy, as he tried to raise himself up in order to look at Geneviève one last time, and as the coachman gathered his reins, another cry emerged from the poor bruised breast.

The cook and the gardener had just leapt forward to catch the little girl in their arms, who, her orders having been carried out, had finally abandoned herself to her sobs.

IV

THAT vacation, suddenly concluded in plaster, had to be prolonged for as long as the fracture demanded. Charlet had no regrets, either for his forced immobility or the interruption of his brilliant studies.

Every day Geneviève came to see him, sat by his bedside, played *nain jaune*, *taquin* or *dames*, or continued reading the prize of honor aloud.

She had not said the slightest word to apologize for the accident, which had happened by her fault, but Charlet was not unaware that she had been confined to bed for a week. He knew with what kindness she now sat with him every day. And when, having recovered from her nervous crisis, she had been able to have herself transported to Beautilleul, the miracle had finally been produced. Without saying anything, Geneviève had leaned over and brushed Charles-Étienne's forehead with her thin lips.

Geneviève loved him a little, in spite of everything. Even if he had to remain lame, Charles-Étienne blessed destiny.

He did not remain lame. By dint of will power, as soon as he was back in Paris, as soon as he resumed his external studies at the lycée, he caught up the time lost.

Geneviève now replied to his letters. He sent her copies of his bulletins. He was happy.

An amity devoid of reckonings was definitively established, one might have said, in the difficult heart of the little Le Rieux. Still reserved and glacial, she directed without having the appearance of doing so the courage of her Charlet. The habit of reading aloud had remained to them. She chose the books from her little library. In the same way that she had revealed her magnificent sang-froid when the accident happened, she now allowed the true tendencies of her young intelligence, directed toward study and meditation, to be seen. During the new vacations, the inseparable pair had a true botanical crisis. The composition of their herbaria absorbed them for entire hours.

"That strange girl," it was said at Bautileul, "has truly had a good influence on Charlet. He, who only used to dream of cuts and lumps, is now the best pupil at the lycée, and even during the vacations he continues his education."

Paradoxically, the child, so fond of sports, as all children become in France, only wanted to hear mention of gymnastics, equitation, cycling and tennis during the Paris season.

※

Fifteen years old . . . strong and agile, blond and virile, he had just completed his baccalaureate with a dispensation. Since the last sojourn in Beautilleul, spurred on by Geneviève in the course of their letters, he had decided definitively to devote himself to the study of ancient Egypt. His father, proud of him, encouraged him, his mother marveled to see a new historian announcing himself in the person of her son, such a handsome adolescent. Jean Masserand's books were at the peak of their success.

In a few months, however, all the happiness of Beautilleul was to be undone.

A prelude to what was to follow, Grandmother Masserand died first, in Paris, as they were about to leave for the summer. It was at her burial that Madame Jean Masserand caught the bronchial pneumonia that carried her off in nine days. Tragically delayed by that double mourning, the three survivors—the overwhelmed grandfather, his devastated son and his sobbing grandson—were floating wrecks, and no longer knew what to decide regarding the departure for the country. Charles-Étienne begged that they go quickly; he needed Geneviève to console him.

"We'll leave on August the second," Jean Masserand said, finally, holding back his tears.

On August the second, war was declared. The residue of misfortunes and upheavals was confounded with the universal catastrophe.

＊

On Armistice Day, nothing any longer remained of the happy family but a father and son harshly treated by the epoch, like all intellectuals after the war. Beautilleul, advantageously sold by its owner, became foreign, no longer anything on the horizon but a lost paradise.

At Bellecour, ruination and death had also done their work. The older of the two messieurs had been sadly extinguished at the blackest point of the war. The other, no longer able to live, for want of money, his fortune having been swallowed up in the various bankruptcies of the period, had put the mortgaged château up for sale. Modestly, almost miserably, he was vegetating in Paris with Geneviève, who was still delicate. The old house-keeper had refused to go with them. Alone among spec-ters, she kept Bellecour until the day when some anony-mous society acquired it in order to found a sanatorium.

Reunited again, in the midst of mournings and col-lapses, Charles-Étienne and Geneviève pursued their singular romance. The common taste they had acquired for study and documentation—or, rather, Geneviève's taste, having become common to both—took them side by side to libraries and museums across Paris. They also frequented art exhibitions and concerts. Together, they educated themselves, a handsome young couple who made the heads of passers-by turn.

A grave student at the School of Oriental Languages, Charles-Étienne had remained, with regard to his com-rade, and in spite of the moustache that he shaved with care, the dreamy, impulsive and timid gamin of old. Since puberty had transformed them into a young man and a young woman, he yearned to declare his amour to her, commenced in the church of Bellecour at the foot of the stained-glass window, and to ask her to be his fiancée; but the cold eyes continued to exercise their magical power.

Geneviève was still the queen of legend to whom one only spoke with a lowered voice. He had not even had the courage to reveal to her the great secret of his child-hood—which he now knew to be a secret—by telling her how, at the age of seven, she had emerged for him from a Bach prelude and a thirteenth-century stained-glass window. He was afraid of her laughter, still the same, and afraid of her eyes, which persisted in only welcoming him at a distance. Never yet had their conversation tipped into sentimentality. In the eleven years that he had been her tremulous companion, he had not ceased to admire and adore her, but he did not know her yet.

That required his departure for the regiment.

Even during the evening of adieux that reunited them one last time in Geneviève's home, beside the slow-burning stove—the old great uncle had been in bed for some time—he could not bring himself to proffer the sacred words to which she might perhaps have listened while making fun of him.

From the depths of Germany, however, where he had been sent, impelled by the despair of exile and the horror of military bullying, also reassured by the distance that separated him from the cold eyes, he finally had the heroism to write to his childhood friend everything that he had not been able to say to her. To keep silent was no longer possible. It was better to know whether she would accept him as a companion of existence or not, whether she had enough affection and esteem for him in her unknown heart to become his wife one day. The Bach prelude, Sainte Radegonde, and what he had suffered since he had known her, all passed into it.

The wait for the response was an unspeakable torture. Hope and discouragement alternated in breaking him. Between a future of perfect happiness and suicide, between yes and no, he oscillated from one minute to the next.

It was in the infirmary, with a forty degree fever, that he finally read Geneviève's letter. And because she replied to him that she had also loved him since the age of seven, he almost died of it.

Twenty-five and twenty-four years old, they were both handsome, both blond, both almost austere in their gravity, but mystically amorous, both cultivated and penniless ...

The academic world congratulated Jean Masserand, who had entered beneath the cupola shortly before; the world in general covered them with good wishes. Behind those compliments and smiles, behind the two pure fiancés, there was backbiting and slander ...

V

GENEVIÈVE raises her eyes. Charlet has just lit a cigarette, the signal for a moment's repose.

A tempest of books and papers overflows the table, spilling on to the chairs and armchairs. One would not guess that such a work-room is a bedroom, that of Charles-Étienne. The divan-bed also serves as a bookshelf, for volumes, journals and pamphlets are piled up on it in the guise of cushions.

The trepidation of Paris is stifled there, amid the documents and the drapes. But for the moment, the cry of the navigation, coming from some tugboat on the nearby Seine, penetrates everything, the clamor of a siren that suddenly creates the atmosphere of a seaport around the books.

Jean Masserand's apartment is too small for two historians. It is necessary to make arrangements not to impede one another.

"We've done good work today," Charles-Étienne declared, stretching himself. "Our book will end up making a fortune some day."

Geneviève considered him disapprovingly. "Why do you say *our* book? It's yours. I'm only a copyist."

"Perhaps, but it's you who had the original idea for the book."

A little morning sunlight passed over their heads. The young man's chestnut hair was suddenly blond; Geneviève's coiled tresses shone like straw.

"Is there any news of old Chables?" she asked.

"Papa tells me that he's getting better; they've said that he can get up today."

"He's truly extraordinary, that fellow. At his age! To have a stroke and get up from it!"

"It appears that it wasn't a stroke. There's no sign of paralysis. Doubtless the heat . . ."

"What an end to a reception, all the same! I can still see him falling at the feet of that princess. The most astonishing thing of all is the way she took it. She left without even asking whether he was dead."

"She must be a fine egotist! She definitely didn't please me."

"Me neither . . ."

They looked at one another, united, as always, by an identical thought. They had already exchanged their impressions since the incident. Troubling, regal, almost too beautiful, that Antinides gave them the impression of a dangerous adventuress.

"Come on, Charlet . . . your cigarette is finished. It'll soon be midday, and I have to go back within the hour. You know that my uncle likes punctuality."

"Why can't you ever have lunch with us? That would simplify everything, since you come back to work with me every afternoon."

"How stubborn you are! I've told you a hundred times that I don't want to leave my uncle to eat lunch alone. His life is already sad enough."

Charles-Étienne looked away momentarily.

"And when we're married?"

A perceptible tremor had altered his voice. He could not talk about their marriage without his heart beating too forcefully.

"First of all, we're not yet close to being married. It's necessary for your book to be published . . . and for it to be successful."

"Oh, Geneviève! Why don't we get married right away?"

She straightened her Medieval little head. Her thin lips did not proffer a word. She had already said everything that she thought about that subject, and declared her will formally never to sponge, when married, on her uncle and her father-in-law. Charlet knew the inflexibility of his fiancée better than anyone. He lowered his nose, crestfallen, as he had when he was small. Always subjugated by her, he reached out for his papers sighing, like an obedient schoolboy.

The silence resumed: their everyday studious silence.

They only looked up at the noise of the door opening. Jean Masserand came in, his pipe in his mouth.

"I'm disturbing you, my children! But someone has just brought me a letter so extraordinary . . . here, read this!"

Geneviève and Charles-Étienne had risen to their feet. Sitting in his son's place, the Academician opened the letter. The two young faces each leaned over one of his shoulders.

Dear Master,

The conversation that I had with your son the other evening at your home interested me so much that I have had an idea, doubtless realizable, which is this:

I am departing in about a month for Egypt, going this year to spend the winter in the palace of Elephantine that I mentioned to you. Why do the young Egyptologist and his fiancée not do me the honor and give me the joy of accompanying me? The documents that I can communicate to your son out there are absolutely unique, and my private museum, which no one knows, would be at his disposal for his research full of unsuspected marvels. I can affirm that they will enrich singularly the knowledge that he already possesses of Pharaonic matters.

The voyage will pose no difficulty for the young people, who will simply take advantage of my yacht and, in Elephantine, of my palace, where their apartments, absolutely independent, will allow them to live as they please without even having to take account of my presence, which will only be manifest when they have need of me as a guide in their studies or their incursions in the land of the great goddess.

Let them not be embarrassed in any way by my hospitality. It is me who will owe them gratitude, only too glad if I can aid a young scholar, the son of an illustrious father, and his collaborator to get to know better the country in which I was born and of which I am proud. I will even confess to you that I have caressed that ambition for many years and had despaired of finding anyone worthy to know my treasures.

If my offer is refused I shall see myself forced to depart alone or to take some banal individuals to keep me company on the voyage and occupy my dwelling, so empty when I have no guests there, and which, like all dwellings, has need from time to time of human respiration in order not to incline dully to ruin.

I am counting on you, Master, to be my intercessor with regard to your two children, of whom I am asking, in sum, a great and noble service.

Hoping for a response that will delight me, I am your very cordial admirer,

Princess Antinides

"Well?" interrogated Jean Masserand, raising his eyes toward the two children. "What do you think of that?"

Charlet, open-mouthed with astonishment, marveling, waited for Geneviève to respond. The idea never occurred to him of thinking something before she had spoken.

Her eyebrows drawn together, Geneviève continued scanning the letter, which remained open on the table.

"How well she knows French, this foreigner," she murmured, "and what magnificent handwriting!"

"That's true," Charles-Étienne hastened to say. In suspense, he awaited the continuation.

"In sum, what do you say?" said Jean Masserand, with a hint of impatience. "Do you accept, or don't you?" His pretty blue eyes were laughing slightly. "Is it a voyage possible for two young people who are not married?" he continued. "What would people think of it in Paris?"

"Oh, if it were only that . . ." said Geneviève.

And the Academician, before that fine scorn for convention, was ashamed of what he had just said. He was never any more at ease than anyone else in the face of his mysterious future daughter-in-law. He tried to recover.

"It's certain that it's very tempting. If everything that she says is true, it's a fortune that she's offering you in exchange for a satisfaction of vanity. And even if she's exaggerating, to go to Egypt, and in such conditions— what a dream!"

"Yes," Geneviève's incisive voice cut in, "but who is she, this woman? Why and how is she so rich? She didn't seem very sympathetic to us. Oh, if it were possible . . . The book that she holds in such esteem could be dedicated to her, and she'd be largely recompensed . . ."

"Yes," said Charles-Étienne, like an echo. "The book could be dedicated to her."

Jean Masserand, increasingly influenced, twisted his gray moustache. "As for knowing exactly who she is, my children, that's not difficult. I'll ask Taillefer for a meeting tomorrow. He knows her quite well. He'll give me all the details."

"Listen, Master . . ." commenced Geneviève. She had just reflected, her long eyebrows were still close together. "It's certain that Charles-Étienne's future might gain a good deal of impetus if we accept this voyage. Egypt is lacking for him, that's evident. It would be absurd to say no to destiny. But if you wish, you could respond initially to the princess by thanking her and asking her to give us a week to think about her offer. Then you can seek information meticulously from Taillefer or elsewhere. We'd like to sacrifice our antipathy, which is perhaps quite unjustified in any case. But if this woman is a shady foreigner, we'll refuse to accept her company and her protection, even if it's in our interest, simply in order to give her the glory of enabling the whole world to know her Egyptian collections. That's what she wants, fundamentally. She knows what she's doing!"

Categorically, she fixed the father and the son alternately, tamed in advance, with her gray eyes.

"Now," she said, "my hat and coat. I'll have to run if I don't want to be late for lunch. We'll talk further this afternoon about all of this."

VI

*M*Y *dear and illustrious friend,*
In order to follow up our conversation of the
other day and complete the information that I've already
been able to give you, this, according to what I've been told
by those who know her best, is the complete dossier on our
very beautiful princess. The greater part has been furnished
to me by the khedival Prince Ahmed, whom you know well
by virtue of having met him in my house, and whose ele-
vated culture and rare common sense you have been able to
appreciate. On the other hand, like me, you have been able
to take account of the fact that the very Parisian Muslim
in question has a rather hard bite, especially when he talks
about his compatriots. We could not, therefore, find a better
informant.

Princess A. was born in Alexandria of an Athenian fa-
ther and mother, more or less ruined aristocrats who came
to Egypt to try to rebuild their fortune. Strangely enough,
that magnificent being is the child of aged parents.

The father, having gone into the cotton trade, traveled
a great deal and always took his wife, who was very beau-
tiful, and of whom he was very jealous. That is why little

Antigone—that is the princess's forename—was brought up far from her parents, at Sacré-Coeur in Paris, which explains her perfect knowledge of our language.[1]

At eighteen years of age, as beautiful as she still is, perfectly educated, learned and artistic, she was married to the son of one of her father's richest correspondents, a South American, and the whole family settled definitively in Brazil. In accordance with old family letters, which the princess allowed him to read, Prince Ahmed thinks that the parents of the beautiful Antigone were very glad to be adopted by her millionaire son-in-law at an age when, no longer able to travel, it was necessary to renounce their means of making a living. The son-in-law was very satisfied himself by his alliance with noble blood, since he was a simple commoner. Her parents died out there and the life of the household continued until the day when Antigone's husband was killed by a fall from a horse. The young widow then returned to Europe. It was in that epoch that she met Ahmed. Her wealth and beauty surrounded her with a host of suitors, but, sage and retired, she did not appear to want to remarry, when Prince Antinides appeared, similarly from Athens.

Ahmed pacha was an intimate friend of the father. He had known the man who was to be Antigone's sole amour since childhood. A young and handsome crazy billionaire, a billionaire via his Californian mother, fond of adventures and yachting, he hastened as soon as he had married

---

1 The name Antigone means "worthy of her parents." It is best-known as the title of Sophocles' tragedy, which ends with Antigone being buried alive in a tomb, where the eponymous heroine commits suicide.

the young widow to take her around the world. Theirs became a life of caprice, of veritable enchantment. The palace of Elephantine was constructed immediately after the marriage, on the site chosen by the princess. Ahmed pacha was invited there immediately. He traveled with the young couple several times. He says that entire fortunes melted in the hands of those two young people, that it is impossible to imagine the luxury in which they lived.

After eighteen months of marriage, however, having gone to India, the unfortunate young Antinides contracted the plague there, which was rife in certain regions into which he had strayed, and he died in a matter of hours in his wife's arms while returning to the palace in Benares where they occupied two apartments.

Imagine the drama, not to mention the general panic caused by such a death. Everything was done to cover the matter up, as you can imagine. The miracle is that the case remained unique in Benares, and that the princess did not contract the horrible disease herself. But she has always said to her old friend Prince Ahmed that she cannot console herself for not having died too. Therein lies the mystery of her strange gaze. That woman, so beautiful and so rich, is inconsolable.

She is now thirty years old. It is six or seven years since her husband died. Ahmed pacha and others have told me that, in spite of her luxury, in spite of the arts and literature in which she tries to interest herself, in spite of the voyages and in spite of the passions that she continues necessarily to provoke everywhere she goes, no existence more desperate than hers has ever been seen. She never remains alone, for fear of yielding to her obsession with suicide. Her desire for death is, it seems, a kind of morbid neurasthenia. But, a firm believer, she intends to retain the courage to live until the end

All those who have approached her closely enough to know her well are astonished by the austerity of her thoughts. They believe that the time is not far off when she will give her fortune to the poor in order to end up in some convent. The alms she gives in all directions are already formidable

Who could suspect such things on seeing her as we have seen her, beautiful to make one quiver—the phrase is not mine—young, prodigiously elegant, well-known in all the interesting milieux of Paris?

Such is, dear friend, the woman who is asking your children for the favor of accompanying her to Egypt. You can see that you can allow them to go with her in complete security. And I can even add that, according to what I have heard, in accepting her offer they would be performing a pure and simple act of charity. All those who love the princess—of whom I am one, alas!—rejoice in thinking that this Valentina Visconti who, less theatrical than the other,[1] hides her despair under such a sparking exterior, can still interest herself in something in this world.

This letter is too long, but my excuse is that it is summoned, I have no doubt, to give you every satisfaction.

Believe, dear and great friend, in my admiration and my amity, always the same.

Taillefer

---

1 Valentina Visconti (1366-1408) was the wife of the murdered Louis de Valois, Duc d'Orléans, subsequently represented by some French Romantic historians and artists as a tragic figure.

＊

The concerns of the voyage had almost entirely put a stop to Charles-Étienne's and Geneviève's labors. The preparations for such a joyful departure made Jean Masserand sigh, anxious and vaguely scandalized, like all today's parents, by the tranquil independence of the new generation. He dare not say what he thought deep down. He dared not admit that, in accord with old Bellecourt, his desire was to have the fiancés accompanied by Madame Leroy, who was keeping futile vigil in an empty château, and would doubtless have agreed to be Geneviève's housekeeper again, the chaperone of the two children confided to her guard.

The fiancés had both gone to see Princess Antinides in order to thank her and to make contact with her before the voyage. They returned from their visit moved, each in accordance with their temperament, by the welcome they had been given in the magnificent private house in which she lived in Paris, in the Place des États-Unis. Now that they knew her story, they understood better everything that had worried them at first about that injured creature: her inwardly-directed gaze, the almost anguishing atmosphere that her unique beauty spread, and the sort of horror that one experienced at her first appearance.

In spite of her thirty flamboyant years, the absolute perfection of her features and the slightest details of her person—embellished, one might have said by the purest gold—that woman was redolent of mourning and death.

Even more than in Jean Masserand's drawing room, she appeared extraordinary to the fiancés in the midst of her familiar décor, wealth managed with a gripping art and personality. Dressed in black when she was at home, draped in long loose garments, she was the most precious object in her collections, ancient and modern.

After a quarter of an hour of intelligent, cordial and curiously documented conversation, she had murmured "*Au revoir*, amiable lovers," on the threshold as she showed them out. And that little speech, after what they knew about her, was simply heart-rending to hear.

"We'll try to distract her, and interest her," Charles-Étienne said, animatedly, while they went home on foot.

But Geneviève said nothing, for her thoughts were going too far in the comprehension of her dolorous sister.

VII

THE beautiful white yacht, so fresh, the color of a
seagull, entered the port of Alexandria smoothly.
On the disembarkation quay, the Muslim horde that lies
in wait for visitors coming from the sea had gathered in
order to rush forward. Arabic cries and battles in the
sun between a hundred porters before the vessel reaches
the shore, the rumor of the impending assault is a great
surprise for those who have not seen it before.

Charles-Étienne and Geneviève, close together, exchanged the pressure of their fingers without speaking.
Everything having been very peaceful during the week
of the crossing, Egypt welcomed them now with this
barbaric shock.

Their eyes dilated in order better to see the furious
exotic silhouettes: the long galabias of the men, their turbans, their tarbooshes, and the few female paupers astray
in the riot, narrow forms of which all that could be seen
were their dark eyes, clad and veiled in black, wearing
gilded cylinders like a hawk's beak on their noses, which
made them resemble divinities of the Nile.

The port and the city appeared frightfully modern, and many European costumes adulterated the Oriental color of the crowd. The little that the fiancés perceived of the land of their dream, however, retained something of that dream even so and they had, as the saying has it, a desire to pinch themselves to see whether it was true.

An order given by the princess, immediately executed, calmed the assailants. The white-clad mariners of the yacht, armed with riding-crops, appeared along the rails, ready to greet with blows anyone audacious enough to risk climbing aboard.

The adroit maneuver of the yacht was concluded. In a moment, it stopped completely. The rocking of the week came to an end, a surprise for muscles that had so rapidly become accustomed to the rhythm of the sea.

During that week, launched toward the unknown, the fiancés had lived new joys and unsuspected enchantments. Throughout the voyage, penetrated by the idea that they had a mission to fulfill, they had striven to surround the princess, trying to make her feel that they were both beside her to care for her broken heart.

The yacht, a floating town house, had furnished the subject of all the initial conversations; Charles-Étienne multiplied his interrogations of an astonished grown-up child.

They had visited the hothouse fitted into the poop, and also discovered the aviary full of dazzling wings, the cushioned kennel where the greyhounds and the Pekinese slept, the aquarium in which the Chinese fish swam: all of the beautiful Antigone's living toys.

Wearily, she smiled at the young couple.

"The crossings are sometimes so long when the sea is as beautiful as it is at this moment. Once, I had a small orchestra . . . but there aren't only flowers and animals aboard. You know. There's also the library . . ."

"Let's go see!"

During the journey through the varnished corridors: "Why is your boat called *Amanit*?"

They had arrived at the door of the library. The princess turned round with a stiff gesture, immobilized before that door. A creature of dream, dressed in the latest fashion, for a few seconds she addressed the young man with a funereal gaze.

"Amanit was the name of a priestess of Hathor," she pronounced, finally.

That unexpected attitude, and also something in her low voice caused Charles-Étienne and Geneviève to shiver. They had to wait until they found themselves alone again in order to communicate the identical thought that, without them being able to divine why, had just traversed their two minds.

Nevertheless, in the library, where they installed themselves on that first afternoon of their voyage, the conversation commenced that was destined to become inexhaustible for the three of them, on the topic of ancient Egypt.

The erudition of the princess was stupefying.

"But Madame," Charles-Étienne observed, after an hour, "how is this possible? You know far more than I do."

The luminous teeth gleamed.

"Perhaps," she said, looking elsewhere. Then, immediately, addressing Geneviève, she rectified: "Don't believe a word of what he says. He's astonished by my petty baggage, but it has now been five years that I've absorbed myself in that, in order to try . . ."

She fell silent. A great shadow passed.

"I understand better now," said Geneviève, after a painful short silence, "the interest you're taking in Charles-Étienne's book."

"Certainly it interests me! Listen to me! It's necessary that it is a *unique* book!"

She enveloped them with the same gaze of amity. Her small, dark and brittle hand, charged with a heavy gold ring, took a pink cigarette from a cup within arm's reach.

"So many errors have been written about Egypt!" Then, negligently, she concluded: "You'll see my collections at Elephantine!"

With that, Charles-Étienne asked questions, passionately. She replied. Geneviève only said a few words from time to time.

That lasted until it was time for tea. The princess rang, and it was in impeccable English that she gave her orders. Then, to the valet who brought her a scarf, she began speaking German with an equal perfection. A little later, it was Italian that she spoke.

"You know all languages!" Geneviève remarked.

"I've traveled so much," she said, simply. Her eyes closed, as if on countless memories.

Charles-Étienne resumed the conversation quickly, in a slightly jesting tone: "Naturally, you know how to decipher inscriptions, Madame?"

No response. She simply darted a glance at him. He did not know what had overwhelmed her. The woman was certainly not always comprehensible.

"Here's the tea!" she exclaimed. And suddenly, she was no longer anything but an almost banal socialite.

While she filled the cups, Charles-Étienne was able to glimpse on Geneviève's face an expression full of things that they would only say to one another later.

It passed so quickly, that week!

A little sea-sickness had sometimes interrupted their cordial intimacy. What did the princess do while her two guests each lay in their cabin with half a lemon between their teeth? She declared that the strongest tempests left her indifferent,

"I was gazing at the sea," she replied, when the swell had passed and the fiancés reemerged. And her face said then what dreams had been hers.

Refined meals staged in the captain's cabin; siestas in the deck-chairs; a visit to the engine room, an explanation of the compass and the wireless apparatus: a hundred distractions cut short the hours. The great cadence of the sea and the hum of the propeller formed a monotonous background to the diversity of the amusements, putting vast punctuations between the words.

"Oh! A chessboard!" exclaimed Charles-Étienne one morning. "I hadn't noticed it before. It's a magnificent museum piece. Do you play, Madame?"

"Yes."

"Let's have a game. I've very strong at chess."

"If you wish," she said, "But you'll be beaten. Even champions can't win against me. That's why it no longer amuses me to play."

"Really?"

It was exact.

"That too?" Charles-Étienne murmured, with a sort of fear, on considering the Machiavellian checkmate that beat him in short order.

The end of October left behind them in France gradually became spring. The mantles were removed.

"In winter, on cold days, it's twelve degrees above zero in Cairo."

Now there was this quay, these gesticulations, these vociferations. A tall majordomo in a dark blue robe with excessively long sleeves, a snowy turban tightly wound, had just come aboard, surrounded by an escort of six gilt-edged and well-dressed Berbers. All of them bowed very deeply, in unison, before the princess, their right hands plunging to the ground and then touching their breasts, their lips and their foreheads: the ceremonial salute of Turkey and Egypt.

"Salaam aleikum," buzzed seven simultaneous voices.

"Oud salaam aleikum," replied the princess.

She continued addressing the majordomo. Her guttural Arabic was accompanied by eloquent grand gestures that she did not have in other languages.

"She also speaks Arabic?" said Geneviève, between her teeth.

"She's formidable!" whispered Charles-Étienne.

And both of them were convinced at that moment that, in spite of the marvels they were going to see, the most exciting aspect of their voyage would be that woman, everything that they were going to discover about that woman.

VIII

"TODAY is the second of November," said Antigone. "Would you like to come to the Christian cemetery with me? I have tombs to visit."

All three of them were walking along the vast stone quay of which Alexandria is proud. The princess had consented willingly, on emerging from the yacht, to those few steps, which delighted the fiancés. The open-topped auto followed meekly behind, the majordomo beside the chauffeur.

On the sea, almost black, as if viscous, in the fashion of a jelly, under the eternal azure of the sky, a little lost sail burst forth, an unexpected whiteness on the horizon. It was necessary to hasten to look at that in order not to be disappointed by Alexandria, which retained nothing of its past but its name.

"It's desperately *up to date*, isn't it?" said the princess, sadly.

"No museum?" asked Charles-Étienne.

"Pooh! Nothing but the modern," she replied—and immediately added: "I mean nothing anterior to the Ptolemies."

At that remark the couple started to laugh, but she retained her somber face. Walking between the two of them, nimbly and as if clad in air, with a scarf beating like a wing around her footsteps, her gait had the rhythm of a sacred ballet. In spite of the little modern hat, in the form of a helmet, her profile, standing out against the dark, hard sea, seemed to reconstitute the ancient Egyptian city.

"How beautiful you are!" said Geneviève, abruptly.

She seemed astonished herself by what she had just said. Always so firm, so glacial, she had spoken as if involuntarily.

The enamel pupils, darted from the corners of the eyelids, considered her in the great shadow of the lashes.

"You too are beautiful, my child."

"Oh, compared with you . . ."

A growl inflated the gilded throat. "But if you knew, my poor child, how fatigued I am by this beauty! It has been such a long time that I've had these great dark eyes, this violet hair, this apricot complexion. It's beautiful, but it's monotonous . . . oh, look . . . like the sea we're skirting, which has been the same blue for more than ten thousand years. One becomes weary of it, you know. Oh, I'd like your pale tresses, your gray eyes that are sometimes mauve; I'd like to be like the grayness of your homeland, less evident and more varied. You're beautiful, I tell you! You resemble closely Anne de Beaujeu.[1] You're more beautiful than I am; you don't have that

1 Anne de Beaujeu (1461-1522) was the Regent of France from 1483-91, one of the most powerful women in Europe. Numerous paintings depict her at prayer, her expression piously serious.

fixity in perfection. Forgive me for saying that. I know full well what I am, don't I? There's no point in making a semblance of not knowing..."

All her features expressed the most frightful despair. She interrupted her march momentarily, also stopping the other two, and continued:

"You're beautiful: fragilely, humanly beautiful. You have beside you the man you love, and who loves you. For you love one another, don't you?" she asked, dully, resuming walking and taking each of the fiancés by the arm.

Now she made them almost run. The passers-by, who had not ceased to turn round, looked at them even more.

"Tell me, tell me how you love one another! You, the boy, how do you love your fiancée?"

Stifled by that haste, Charles-Étienne dared not reply. He tilted his head in order to try to look at Geneviève, dragged like him on the other side of the princess. Certainly, Geneviève also had the impression of a dangerous crisis of neurasthenia.

"How do you love her? Reply to me! Reply to me!"

Finally, he decided. With the most tranquil inflection: "Madame, I love her like myself."

"That's not true!"

She had cried that as if outraged, stopping again. She went on, excitedly: "One never loves anyone like oneself. A man never loves a woman like that. He loves her *for* himself, not for *her*."

She went to the parapet. Turning her back on the sea, her head bowed, she stared into the void. The two young people looked at her anxiously.

"Madame," Charles-Étienne commenced, with an obstinate coldness, "I love Geneviève like myself. No! I love her more than myself, that's the truth. We've told you a little about our childhood. It's not only a matter for me of desire, youth or anything that can pass. Nothing can ever take me away from Geneviève. She is my soul, more than my soul . . . she is . . ."

He passed his hand over his eyes. "Pardon me. I've never said as much, even to her. She has no need for me to say it to her. She knows. For my love for her is such that I never talk about it, any more than one talks about one's love of oneself."

Geneviève had taken him by the wrist, astonished by that concentrated vehemence. Perhaps she was trying to make him shut up.

Antigone, quitting the void, examined them both with her most incomprehensible gaze. Such energy filled the floral eyes of young Masserand that they were almost hard.

A group that was following the quay brushed all three of them, bringing them back to reality. A delightful smile appeared then on the face of the princess. Her contracted features relaxed

"How lovely youth is!" she sighed, in the tone of a very old woman.

With a weary and affectionate gesture, her hands alighted on their shoulders, to the right and the left. And as if she had forgotten everything, abruptly, indifferent and detached: "Come! We'll get into the car now. It's absolutely necessary that I go to the cemetery before lunch."

At the cemetery there were Muslims with watering cans who were inundating the stones of the Christian tombs.

"Why . . . ?" asked Charles-Étienne.

"It represents the tears of the family," said Antigone. "These banabacs are paid to perform this service every year."

Slightly agitated, she searched for her tombs. She found one, then a second, and then a third. She gazed at them one after another, immobile and upright. Perhaps she was praying. Why had she not brought flowers?

Retreating to one side, the fiancés interested themselves in an old lady in a small black hood, very provincial and very European, who was gardening around a tomb, as one does in French cemeteries. When she had disposed her bouquets neatly, dusted the marble and adjusted the crown of pearls, they saw her open the umbrella she had brought, even though the African sun was shining ardently. She crouched on her heels, arranged her skirt around her, straightened the pleats of her mantle, directed the umbrella in such a fashion as to shelter her from the heat, and, having installed herself thus, she started howling like a she-wolf amid floods of tears.

Antigone returned to the young couple. She responded to their gaze of interrogative stupefaction calmly: "She's weeping for a member of her family who died a long time ago, since she has no crepe. It's the day of the dead; she's obeying the protocol."

They remained where they were, unable to take their eyes off the aged mourner.

"One would think that she were putting a rhythm into it," Geneviève remarked

"Naturally. She's sobbing in cadence. She might be Catholic, but she's an Egyptian. You'll soon take account of the fact that nothing is done in Egypt without a certain musicality. That goes back a long way. It was already the case in the time of the Pharaohs."

"Is it possible . . . ?" exclaimed Charles-Étienne.

"In spite of appearances," the princess went on, "nothing changes in Egypt. Remember that."

She took a few steps toward the exit and concluded solemnly, looking into the distance ahead of her: "Nothing changes anywhere, in fact."

They did not react to that bizarre affirmation. They had already been able to observe that, with regard to the strange Antinides it was sometimes good to put into practice the popular saying with regard to the mad: It is necessary not to contradict them.

They followed her in silence. She glided between the sunlit tombs, tall, straight and slim, holding her noble helmeted head high, leaving behind her a light current of unknown perfumes.

It was only in the auto that she spoke again.

"We're going to lunch now; and if you're not too tired, we'll get into the auto again immediately afterwards. We need to reach Cairo as quickly as possible, the Sphinx, the Pyramids, the Nile and the desert, in order to make you forget Alexandria. However, if it's all right with you, we'll only stay there a few days. We'll return later. I'm in haste to receive you at Elephantine."

And in her magnificent eyes, which had become fixed again, Charles-Étienne, sitting facing her, saw mysteries and marvels rising.

IX

As soon as one sets foot in it, European Cairo reveals its luxury and pleasure. A happy idleness trails with the heat between the white palaces and the modern buildings that are gradually substituting themselves for the Islamic city, the color of terra cotta, once so appropriate to the indigo of the sky and the fire of the sun.

Among the increasingly grave crimes of progress—an international vandalism—it is only just to recognize that sometimes the effort of certain contemporaries strives to replace the demolished beauty with new beauty. A hotel like that of Heliopolis, for example, which has something in it of a mosque and a temple of Isis, is not devoid of refinement and magnificence. It was there that Antigone Antinides decided to stay for the three days that she deigned to grant to Cairo.

"With the auto we'll be everywhere in an instant. Heliopolis is now a suburb of Cairo."

Installed in full enchantment, each having a room as big as an apartment, Charles-Étienne and Geneviève scarcely had time to respire the desert atmosphere that surrounded the vast palace of an Arabian tale, initially constructed all alone in the midst of sands, which a town has since come to surround. The day after their arrival, at nine o'clock in the morning, they were on foot.

The princess had not submitted any program to them. They did not know where they were going.

In the midst of all they saw that was so new to them—the Orient in detail, colors, odors and sounds that astonished their senses, avid not to miss anything—they touched one another's arms incessantly, retaining exclamations. Their hostess being taciturn that morning, they dared not trouble her silence.

The auto went along narrow streets where the people scarcely disturbed themselves to let it pass. Muslim nonchalance is the same everywhere. However, accidents are very rare in the supple and slow crowd, which opens and closes like water.

"It's here!" the princess said, suddenly. She was now feverish, as if in haste.

They followed her. Stone steps were climbed, the flank of an edifice that they did not know to be a citadel.

"Look!"

They did not guess immediately. There were minarets in the foreground. In the distance, in the immense extent, felted with golden dust, like all of Egypt, and through which the fresh clarity of the Nile snaked, between buildings and palm trees reduced to the state of toys by the distance, a few geometrical silhouettes followed one another on the edge of the horizon, obscure in the general tonality, which is that of the pelt of a lion.

"This time, this is Egypt; what do you think of it?"

After only a few seconds, Geneviève was the first to understand. Her fist over her mouth, she exclaimed: "The Pyramids!"

A little snigger made her shudder.

"Ah! Finally!"

Antigone's imperious finger pointed at the Nilotic panorama. Her proud voice almost in a whisper, emphasized: "You see! There is the Greatness! There is the Supreme! There is the Horizon!"

She gave the impression of offering it to them in the palm of her hand. Her curls, with blue reflections, thrown back over her nape, fluttered in a breath of wind around her narrow felt bonnet. She was braced proudly, a wingless Victory above the valley haunted by the sublime past. And the two poets who were looking at her both sensed how much grandeur her presence added to the Egypt that she was revealing to them.

Not another word could be said. All three fell silent, religiously.

The eternal hawks that circle in the Egyptian sky, living hieroglyphs, were whistling high above their heads, untiringly on the lookout for prey. For thousands of years they had been circling above the living as if they were waiting for them to die, in order to swoop down on their cadavers. Some descended so low that the fan of their wings was perceptible. They had no fear, sometimes, of swooping down on Arab children in order to carry away the piece of bread that they were holding in their hand.

A harsh and fixed sunlight petrified the landscape. Egypt is one long desert where it happens that the Nile gives birth to a paradoxical fecundity on each of its banks: the "black country," said the ancients. And if the true inhabitants feel the need to dress in dark blue and black, it is because they know instinctively that vivid colors are condemned, in Egypt, to be devoured by light, like everything else.

Charles-Étienne and Geneviève contemplated it, their hearts slightly constricted. In the same fashion as all those who gaze and who have gazed at it meditatively, they felt for a moment that they were arrested on the brink of eternity.

They were unable to go as far as the end of their meditation. Egypt, for them had thus far only been books, documents, engravings, files and display cases, the mummies and statues in the Louvre. The sun, the air, the sky and the blond powder that hovered everywhere like a luminous mist; the whistling of the hawks overhead; the respiration of the living city around them; the special taste that the light wind had, were all redolent with the breath of the dead things of their studies. They had a desire to squeeze one another's hand, to sigh, perhaps to weep.

How long did that contemplation last?

"Let's go!" ordered Antigone suddenly, as if fleeing.

And without speaking, heads bowed, they went down the steps behind her.

"It's necessary, all the same, to go and see the tombs of the Caliphs, the mosque of Omar, El Azhar, old Cairo, the Mokkattam . . . Tomorrow, Sunday, we'll go to the Coptic mass. The orthodox church is full of the purest Egyptian types. And then, Geneviève will be very amused to be parked up above, behind the grille, with the Coptic women, who are veiled like Muslims. One could believe it was the time of Theodora . . ."[1]

A feeble smile accompanied those words, the first ones pronounced since they had climbed back into the vehicle. Satisfied with their long silent emotion, the princess looked at them both with eyes that she rarely had—which is to say, almost human.

"And the Sphinx?" asked Charles-Étienne timidly.

"The Sphinx? You'll see it, but at my time and in my fashion."

The smile elongated on her mouth, that violet stain in the green pallor of her mask. A diamond light filtered blackly between her curved lashes. Her head in the light, rocked by the motion of the vehicle, she seemed to be the Sphinx herself—in the time when the Sphinx gazed.

Two days of fatigue. A feverish rush toward everything she had announced. Then, into the desert on the third day, mounted on requisitioned camels, surrounded by Berbers on horseback, as the sun descended over the end of their excursion, as the two fiancés were wondering where they were being taken to finish, abruptly, they were before the Sphinx

---

1 Theodora (c500-548) was the wife of Justinian I and Empress of the Eastern Roman Empire.

The princess had not wanted to take the usual route at the usual hour, had not wanted the Mena House or the classic tourists' trip.

The clamor of the young couple recompensed her for her amicable ruse.

Increasingly disengaged from the sand that buried it, it is there, broken-nosed blind and monstrous. A vestige of rouge remains on its cheek, swept by the centuries. Its thick mouth, forever sealed, retains the supreme response that it will never give. Perhaps in another thousand years it will become again the rock that it must have been before receiving life, at the same time as the form inexplicably imagined by prodigious predecessors.

All three had ended up setting foot before the stone beast.

"This is Abul Hole," the princess saluted.

"What are you calling it?"

"I'm calling it by its Arab name: the Father of Terror."

"The name suits it well," said Geneviève in a low voice.

"Did you see?" Charles-Étienne remarked. "There are traces of color remaining on its face!"

Antigone almost shrugged her shoulders. "Naturally! It was entirely painted."

"You believe so?"

She opened her mouth to reply, but remained silent.

"And to think that we'll never know exactly what the ancient Egyptians wanted to say in sculpting it!"

Charles-Étienne shook his head, while moving around in order to see the Thing from different angles.

The princess and Geneviève had sat down on the edge of the excavation opened in the sand to disengage the Father of Terror, which forms the formidable abode in which it lies as if it were its claws that had hollowed it out.

"Why do you think that no one knows what they wanted to say?" the princess interrogated, suddenly. "It isn't so difficult to understand."

"Ah! Tell us, then Madame! In this sunset, in this silence, it would be good to hear you. You give such an impression of being of the same race!"

"But I am of the same race!" she retorted.

"You were born in Egypt, but you're Greek, it seems to me."

She bit her lips. "That's true . . . I sometimes forget. But my childhood was Egyptian, was it not? So . . ."

"We're listening to you, Madame," murmured Geneviève, advancing her narrow face, in which the gray eyes were magnified in the dusk. "Give us your interpretation. It can't be other than very interesting."

Antigone turned toward Geneviève in order to smile at her, a smile that lingered throughout a silence. Then, leaning on her elbow in the sand, she commenced, negligently: "My interpretation? The Sphinx has the body of an animal and the head of a god. It was named, in any case, the God of the Two Horizons. Before the construction of the pyramids, it . . . but let's pass on. The Two Horizons! Toward one is directed its bestial rump, and toward the other its royal head. You don't understand?"

She straightened up. Her voice became almost vehement.

"Its head is looking forever toward the dawn, its rump is turned forever toward the sunset. The dawn is light, thought, the ideal, belief, arts, music, laws, progress and survival. The sunset is night, barbarity, evil, bestiality, regression, annihilation and death. It therefore signifies all of human history. The dawn bathes our head, but we don't only have that head. We also have that bestial rump, with its sex, and that is the part of the night. This means that, in spite of all our efforts, we will never be completely divine. It means that we will always be subject to the law of the End and the Recommencement. It means that, if one epoch launches itself forward, another recoils. That is the monotonous rhythm that all nature offers us: morning, afternoon, evening, night; spring, summer, autumn, winter. It's the cycle from which we cannot emerge, the serpent that bites its own tail, the symbol of India. What can change under the geometrical firmament? Humans imagine that they are advancing, but they are circling. Humans don't change. They will always need Hell and Paradise. Religions or principles are renewed, but the base is the same, Hell for the rump of the sated beast, Paradise for the head of the sad god. The Sphinx is us, since the world has existed; it is you . . . it is me."

She fell silent. The two young people were still listening.

Then a surprising hilarity rose up in the deepening shadow. The princess tilted her head back in order to laugh more at her ease.

"Do you truly believe that you've made progress, you others, with your modern inventions? Ha ha! It's a dawn, yes, but one that repeats so many others. Your electricity, for example—oh, your electricity! Do you think, by chance, that it wasn't known here, in the time when the Sphinx was painted? How, then were the lives of the pharaohs designed in miniature on the walls of the tombs buried in the seven darknesses of the Valley of Kings. Your light-bulbs—what a fine barbarity! You . . ."

Her laughter stopped dead. She had stood up so quickly that they did not see her get up. Urgently, seriously, already departed, she cried: "My children, let's hurry back. The night is here!"

X

THE mimesis that made the color of ancient Cairo is respected here. Yellow, like the soil of Elephantine, the immense construction isolated in its gardens crowns and calms a landscape in which the rocks all around the turbulent Nile are, so willfully, deformed sketches of the Sphinx. Simplicity, straight lines, severe ornamentation, the burnt tone of the walls and their height would encourage belief in some ancient Saracen fortress were it not for the bougainvilleas, a Tunisian importation, climbing up to all the windows, were it not for those gardens of palm trees, so curiously designed, a part of which is steeped in the first cataract, partly surrounding the Antinides palace, and were it not for the admirable fountain that spreads its pearls and diamonds amid the marvelously reconstituted Pharaonic mosaics, the precious center of the interior courtyard.

"But it's a city!" Charles-Étienne had cried, at the moment when the auto was engulfed by the decorated shadow of the palm trees.

A swarm of servants circulated, male and female, all African: mulattos, negroes and Berbers, more or less dark faces, mingled with the Copts and white Muslims of Egypt and elsewhere, all Oriental, some in roseate, pistachio green and lemon yellow robes, others in dark blue mantles, some striped, some red and braided with gold, almost all the women clad in black and veiled in black. A few negroes had the turquoise blue turbans that one hardly ever sees except at the festivals of the Mouled, among the Sayed and the Bakri, in Cairo, during the seventeen religious nights on which the birth of the prophet is celebrated.

Doubtless, many of those people, simple figurants, were only there for the charm of their costumes: the pastel shades of the Tunisians; the south Moroccan ephebes clad in linen and wearing silver pendants in one ear; a few Syrian Bedouins with tricolor boots and uncovered faces; and two or three Khroumire women with tattooed cheeks, ankles laden with silver bracelets, bare feet dyed with henna and heads heavily draped and ligatured with necklaces and amulets. There was even a Turkish eunuch, a tall black man going gray at the disdainful lips, circulating cane in hand, charged with containing the effusions of that variegated population.

As in the mosque of El Azhar, all of Islam was represented there.

Salaams burst forth everywhere when the auto stopped outside the gigantic principal door. No atmosphere more purely exotic had ever struck European senses. The princess repelled that petty crowd with a gesture, the members of which wanted at any price to kiss her hands or the hem of her dress, amid exclamations of welcome. Geneviève was less well able to defend herself.

Even Charles-Étienne, utterly bewildered, did not know how to prevent those men and women from putting their lips to the flap of his linen jacket.

The old eunuch ran forward, distributing blows, and the guttural insults with which he accompanied them were uttered in a voice more highly-pitched than that of a boy.

After such a bustle and din, the silence into which they entered as they crossed the threshold of the palace was as gripping as a shock.

A demi-obscurity reigned with coolness under the ceiling lost in the somber heights. Gold glistened, dully, in the corners. The large flagstones over which they advanced were cut in all directions by attenuated woolen carpets. A new fountain was singing elsewhere. A hint of incense trailed, as in every truly Egyptian dwelling.

Where are we? thought the two fiancés, trying to take one another by the hand.

"You'll be taken to your apartments immediately," said Antigone. "Here, Mohammed, Fituri, Salah! You, Mohammed, are going to . . ."

She continued to give her orders in Arabic.

Preceded by three gliding phantoms, the two young people went via rooms, at the painted faience of which they did not have time to gaze, to the weighty iron cage of a very modern elevator. On the second floor they found four black servants of both sexes waiting for them, who spoke sufficient French to eliminate all embarrassment from the service.

It was three o'clock in the afternoon.

"We'll meet again for tea," the princess had said, as she handed them over to their conductors.

And both of them, accepting the adventure, allowed themselves to be led separately, each to one of the corners of the immense floor.

Their two apartments, each composed of four or five rooms, were as distant from one another as possible, a supreme sentiment of decency on the part of the princess.

The seal of the old Orient, an arrangement not reminiscent of anything, the craziest luxury in the most determined sobriety, the most perfect comfort in the strangest of décors: they found all of that ready for them, everything that they did not see or sense at first before the sight that their windows, open over the cataract, overlooked.

They were obliged to the same exclamation for the tormented Nile between its tormented banks, an almost bald landscape stupefied in the light, which gives the impression so well of being as far as possible from everything that one has ever known.

Silently, while they lingered in contemplation of that, each of them regretted the absence of the other, their trunks having been opened and unpacked, their effects arranged and their baths prepared.

When they were refreshed, massaged, perfumed, reposed, and clad in garments that they found, they were each conducted by one of the phantoms to a small, intimate room on the ground floor, where their hostess was waiting for them. She was extended in the middle of a heap of leather cushions, having resumed black clothing, lost in the shadow, stranger than all of her strange domain.

Around her were low, precious, unclassifiable items of furniture, moist roses in pots with turquoise sides, a few objects of Egyptian excavations, her perfume, which was no longer the same, one of the greyhounds lying on the black marble floor tiles, one of the Pekinese lying at her feet, and, hanging from a low golden ceiling, a golden cage in which a black parrot was circling.

Adjacent to that little room full of beneficent and light gloom there was another room even smaller, only furnished with bare marble, having nothing for a back but empty space, open air, a view over the Nile: an opening that could be blocked by heavy Asiatic curtains, now massed to the right and the left in their heavy rings.

Two Berbers came in with trays bearing the tea.

"Come, my children, come! We're going to have tea."

"Madame . . ." commenced the lovers, their mouths full of exclamations.

She divined that they were about to thank her ecstatically. "No!" she said, with her grandiose air of weariness. "We don't have the time. You're well installed, I know, and I'm very satisfied by it; but this will be our last meeting for two weeks, at least. I warned you that you would only see me in order to serve you as a guide. You have no need of me for the moment. You're going to make contact with Elephantine, organize your life, work, stroll—in sum, do whatever you wish. There are people here to prepare all the excursions that tempt you. And when you resume the voyage, acclimatized, the three of us will see one another from time to time."

She hastened to reassure them: "Don't believe that I'm abandoning you. I have so many things to show you, things that are indispensable for your work. But it's not necessary to hurry, is it?"

While speaking, she occupied herself with the tea, having them served by the Berbers, offering them Arabic delicacies, European cakes, rose jam and sweet wines.

"If you want to hear music," she continued, "in addition to the wireless, there is everything you need here. I have Arabic musiciennes. And if you want to make it yourselves, there are all instruments at your disposal. The library is yours; the games room is yours; the tennis court is yours. You have horses in the stables and autos in the garages. My boats and oarsmen are waiting for you. There's no danger with them. In order to be patient until we go up the Nile in a dahabeah, you can risk yourselves without fear on the cataracts."

Her mouth was smiling; her eyes remained tragic.

"Furthermore, I've established a program for you. My Arab steward has it in his hands. You can follow it if it suits you. But above all, make yourselves at home. My entire house is at your disposal."

Nibbling and sipping, they tried in vain to put in a word of gratitude. She stopped them every time, imperiously, with her hand.

They were able to talk briefly about the Nile, the light, the costumes, the gardens, the wealth, the comfort and the coolness of the palace, but when they had pushed away their plates gently, they thought it as well to get up.

"*Au revoir!*" she said, in an extenuated voice. "We'll see one another again soon."

Charles-Étienne brushed with a kiss the light fingers where the gold ring was resplendent. Geneviève shook the other hand.

With a final bow they left, respectfully preceded by the living shadows that had brought them.

And such were their first impressions of the Antinides palace where, in spite of everything that had been offered to them, they both felt mortally out of place.

XI

AFTER two days, they had reorganized joy.

Side by side in the midst of strange marvels, the sentiment of their exile, so far from everything that had thus far constituted the atmosphere in which they loved one another, only served to unite them more. Each of them was for the other the homeland, the family and the quotidian. Their childhood, still so close, returned to their eyes and their lips while they undertook excursions on horseback, guided by two or three taciturn draped cavaliers, while they took a turn in a boat on the cataract at the whim of an enigmatic and somber Muslim navigator, while they played tennis together, while they rocked in hammocks, or while, remaining indoors, they played the piano, played a game of billiards or arranged their books and put their papers in order.

The heat often inconvenienced Geneviève. Charles-Étienne supported it better. However, neither of them seemed ready to set to work. The living Egypt they had respired deflected them from the one they had studied until now, a mummy in its mysterious bandages.

"We're on vacation!" said Charlet, laughing.

They amused themselves. Everything was a novelty for them, the interior as well as the exterior. Their meals, served by bronzed figures, the siesta that they had ended up adopting, and the unusual opulence in which they allowed themselves to live, were a fairy tale abruptly entered into their destiny.

More than two weeks passed thus. Then, gently insinuated into their hearts, an anxiety commenced to make itself manifest. Only Charles-Étienne let it show.

Were they ever going to see the princess again, who had become perfectly invisible? In what part of the palace was she resident, and what was she doing?

Isolated in the middle of an entirely Oriental world, they felt far from everything, abandoned in luxury, heat and idleness. They measured the distance that separated them from Paris and the time they would have to wait to receive responses to the letters addressed to their relatives.

When they found themselves in one or other of their apartments, their day was over.

"In sum, we're the only Europeans here . . ." Charles-Étienne observed.

"Yes . . . so what?"

"Nothing . . . but it is, nevertheless, a rather curious sensation."

"I don't say the contrary . . ."

"And if the princess . . ." Charles-Étienne hesitated momentarily. "What if the princess has gone?"

"Gone? You're losing your sang-froid, Charlet."

"Fortunately, you're here, Geneviève. What if she really has gone?"

"Gone . . . or isolated herself . . ."

"You're right. She certainly isn't normal,"

"That, no. However, I still believe that she's only neurasthenic. Let's let the whim pass. She'll reappear one of these days. In any case, she warned us."

"That's true—but even so, what's happened to us is odd."

"Nothing's happened that isn't magnificent. Of what do we have to complain?"

"I don't know . . ."

"Come on, Charlet. It's necessary for us to get to work. The vacation has lasted long enough. Look, tomorrow morning, we'll resume the chapter that was interrupted in Paris."

"I don't have any enthusiasm."

"I'll give you some. We haven't come to Egypt to play games. We've come here to work, and we're going to work."

"How strong you are, Geneviève!"

"How weak you are, Charles-Étienne!"

"My beloved . . ."

"Come on! Don't get soppy. Bonsoir. Sleep well. Sleep like a log. I'm there at the other end of the gallery, and I'll sleep well too."

"You aren't afraid of anything, Geneviève?"

The gray eyes had their great cold gaze. "Don't be an imbecile, Charlet."

"Pardon me! Oh, what would I be without you?"

"Come on, bonsoir!"

"Bonsoir. I adore you . . ."

One morning, when they were sitting at Charles-Étienne's desk and the latter was tracing a few lines, limply, that were immediately crossed out, and yawning under the severe gaze of Geneviève, they turned round with a frisson. The princess was behind them.

By what door had she entered? They were never able to explain it.

"To work!" she exclaimed, without saying bonjour. "It's today that we're going to begin the study of my personal museum."

The fiancés had stood up in order to salute her. She did not extend her hand or smile.

"Come!" she said, imperiously.

And without a word they followed the light black robe that preceded them rapidly through the vestibules and galleries.

She took her time to open the bronze door that comported a long secret.

A tortuous staircase descending underground had brought them there. There was no electricity. Antigone, furnished with a pocket lamp—or, rather, a powerful miniature searchlight—illuminated their march.

The door finally yielded and closed again on the three of them.

"Voilà!"

The princess raised her light. They were in a rectangular crypt, rather small, the entire depth of which was fitted out like an ancient Egyptian dwelling in which someone had not ceased to respire. There was an abundance of furniture, and carts worn down to the point of being threadbare. On a low table, however, gleams were cast by the riches accumulated there in gold and jewels. A few paintings of sacred individuals were hanging, in a perfect state of conservation, save for creases where the warp showed through. A pharaonic harp, the gilt of which had not disappeared, had freshly tightened strings, as if it could still be played. A hundred pieces of pottery were lined up. There was no trace of millennial burial on their neatly colored flanks. A vast golden lamp fell from the vault, of a model unknown to Egyptology.

Isolated against the somber wall, almost at the entrance, a throne of precious stones shone like a nocturnal illumination. Above it were arranged a succession of respondents, turquoise blue or red terra cotta, thirty or forty vases of various sizes, metal, onyx or other precious substances. A sequence of intact stones was framed, engraved with hieroglyphs.

The princess went to pull a curtain facing the throne, at the same time as she extinguished her lamp. A chapel appeared in which—the principal fascination of the place—its feet covered by a flood of flowers cultivated in the royal greenhouses of the Antinides palace, surrounded by glowing little glass night-lights, a horned statue of Hathor stood, frightening and gigantic, the smooth bronze of which, enriched with gold, shone softly. It was as if the goddess had never been eroded by the slow labor that wears away the most imperishable idols in the eternal night of buried ruins.

A hundred treasures that they could not make out clearly were agglutinated, suspended in the occult darkness of the chapel. Perhaps there were masks, and perhaps other things: censers, amulets, ex-votos and offerings. Two mummified rams were lying to the right and the left of the statue, covered with a golden crust. A few statues of smaller dimension were perceptible, aligned in the semi-darkness, two of which, in painted stone, enormous, like the rest, were strangely pure, without any stigmata, without any of the wounds or the leprosy that disfigure the vestiges painfully extracted from the entrails of digs.

Their hands over their mouths, the fiancés gazed.

The princess lit her lamp again, placed it in a convenient corner, and came back toward them. An expression of triumph exalted her splendid visage, ordinarily fixed in the drama of mourning.

"Can you take account of what you're going to extract from all this?" she exclaimed, finally.

Laughter passed through her mouth while her eyes remained severe.

"And you haven't yet seen everything! I have papyri, Charles-Étienne! I'll decipher them for you. I know them by heart, like all these hieroglyphs that you see on the stones."

"Oh!" said Charles-Étienne, suffocated

"You know how to read them, then?" exclaimed Geneviève. She was standing still, her eyebrows furrowed.

"Yes."

"That's unusual," they murmured, at the same time.

"You haven't yet perceived that with me you're in the unusual?"

They looked away. A singular malaise inhibited their respiration. Where were they going, and to whom were they talking?"

A skip on the part of the princess awoke them from their dream. They had never seen her so lively.

"Here!" she said, almost gaily. "Look at these little sandals. Good. Turn them over now, and see what there is on the soles! You see these persons, here a man, and there a woman—portraits of enemies! One walks on them all day long, you see!"

Her eyes darted a black flame. "It's intoxicating!"

She took back the precious painted pair.

"We'll come back to the goddess in a little while. Don't look at her any longer! Anyway, I'd prefer to close the curtain again. There! At this moment, I'm amusing myself. Hold on! That urn . . . ! You won't see its like in any collection. And this necklace! I'll tell you what it signifies. And this little bottle . . . ha ha! . . . if you suspected . . . you didn't imagine all this, did you?"

Passing on, she stopped abruptly in a corner.

"And this! It's particularly interesting for you. Do you know what it is?"

They advanced meekly and saw a crude little wooden seat of archaic form, its corners blunted by the centuries, but the rusticity of which was surprising among so many imperial riches.

"I kept it," said Antigone, "because it's signed. And then, I love that it's here, because . . . we're no longer in

Egyptology. In any case, one day I'll open the gulfs of these lateral cellars for you. There's an entire museum there too, a museum of all times and all lands . . . are you looking for the signature on my stool? No, you won't find it without me. It's two Hebrew letters engraved with a knife. Wait I'll bring the lamp. There . . . look. Do you see? It's almost effaced but, in sum . . ."

"Yes, yes," said Charles-Étienne. "I can see something . . . but I don't know Hebrew. Do you know it, Madame?"

"Of course!" she snapped; then she immediately said, by way of correction: "That is to say . . . a little . . ."

The two young people nudged one another imperceptibly.

"And whose is that signature?" asked Geneviève, a trifle belatedly.

In the light of the lamp that she was holding aloft, she showed them the most natural expression.

"Jesus Christ," she said. "He was a carpenter, but on occasion he fabricated furniture for Yousoff's poor clientele."

She did not appear to perceive that the two fiancés had taken a step back.

"But let's occupy ourselves with your book," she continued. "Everything here, Charles-Étienne and Geneviève, is at your disposal, and I'm here to explain everything to you. And you know, *no one* has ever seen what I'm enabling you to see."

They no longer dared to respond. After what she had just said to them, they were suddenly hesitating between mystification and folly. They were now wondering, before the accumulation of unpolluted splendors that were shining in their eyes, whether, reinforced by millions, this Jewess who was hiding her race had not had copies made of the things of ancient Egypt, or had her own imaginations executed.

She divined something of what they were thinking. A formidable and mute hilarity made her immense pupils fulgurant.

"You believe they're reconstitutions, impostures? Poor children! You have false intelligence, like all those who call themselves scholars, because you've never seen anything but broken pieces of the old Egypt drawn from oblivion by groping pickaxes. But when you've touched, examined, and studied with a magnifying glass, you're good enough Egyptologists to recognize the mark of the past. No, there's no trickery here, my children!"

"But the origins, Madame!" Geneviève ventured. "How and where have you found all this?"

It was toward Charles-Étienne that she turned her inexplicable gaze, suddenly harder than stone.

"I think that you'll know one day," she pronounced, slowly.

XII

"HAVE you got that, Geneviève?"
       "Just a second!"
    "Don't dictate so quickly!" said Antigone. "You can
see that she can no longer keep up with you."

The work table, immense and practical, was offered
to their three avidities. In the midst of papers, books and
documents, they gave the impression, seated and leaning
over facing one another, their arms extended, of swim-
ming in an ocean of intellectuality.

The authenticity of the treasures in the crypt having
been easily recognized, the fiancés, intoxicated by labor,
no longer quit that room in Charles-Étienne's apartment,
where they had resumed their passionate collaboration
with an unbridled enthusiasm.

The princess, incessantly installed by their side, aided
them with all her science, much more profound than
they had imagined at first.

Three question marks remained in suspense in
their minds. By virtue of what sequence of miraculous
circumstances had she been able to compose that un-
equaled museum and bring together those writings and

engraved stones, everything from which they were now about to extract a sensational work? She had not said another word about that enigma. On the other hand, why had she never revealed that crypt, which would have revolutionized the world? Finally, on the day when she had delivered her marvels to them, why show them that ridiculous stool and pronounce those disquieting words? A simple pleasantry? Mental derangement?

The impression of latent madness sensed several times in her presence, now disappeared before the perfect lucidity and the stupefying authority with which she directed their research. They sensed that she was, henceforth, the light of their book, and that, without her, they would fall back into their miserable gropings.

A singular respect and a bewildered gratitude were born in them for that fabulous woman, who had taken them under her protection, and, in addition to her sumptuous hospitality, was giving them more than one fortune.

The letters that they sent to Paris reflected their joy. They did not talk about returning there. They knew that in addition to the inexhaustible Elephantine, Cairo awaited them for a second time, and also Luxor, the Valley of Kings, Philoe and other places.

"Apart from the temples, they will only be voyages of comparison, you understand, my dear children. You have everything necessary here. Even when you see the tomb of Tutankhamen, you will take account of the fact that it is only old repetition by comparison with what I have shown you."

The first of January arrived very quietly without them paying any heed to it. The letters from Jean Masserand and Monsieur de Bellecour commenced to manifest some anguish. Were the two stolen children going to let their elders celebrate the new year without them?

They laughed at that candid demand, and then responded that it was necessary not to count on them for some time. There followed all the desirable good wishes, as well as a new explosion of joy on the part of Charles-Étienne. He and Geneviève would only return to Pars in order to be married, sure now of great publicity for their considerable work, an unprecedented event.

Meanwhile they wondered themselves, young Masserand with child-like eyes, by means of what dazzling fête at the Antinides palace the first day of the new year would be celebrated.

Christmas had passed unperceived. Saint Sylvester's Day surprised them by its aspect of an ordinary day. They finally told one another that the princess's mourning did not permit any rejoicing. However, on the morning of the first of January, when she came into the work room as she entered every day, they ran to her.

"Happy new year, Madame!"

She considered them, surprised.

"What? It's the first day of the year? I didn't know. All my people are Muslims; so, it isn't . . ."

She came to sit down at the table and went on: "Here in Egypt, I always forget what era we're in . . ."

They suddenly saw again an expression that they already knew.

"I'd like to be able to forget, truly," she growled, her eyebrows furrowed terribly.

Leaning on her elbows, her cheeks in her hands, she looked straight ahead somberly and spoke.

"On the day when they crucified the Rabb,"[1] she commenced, "they crucified all the gods with him . . ."

Several times she repeated, like an echo: "All the gods . . ."

She continued: "The Word made flesh? Sacrilege! Divinity ought to remain hidden forever. As soon as it speaks, walks, eats, drinks, shows hands, feet and eyes, everything that humans have in order to live, as soon as that which possessed all the stars of the firmament shrinks to have only five senses, humans immediately begin to address it familiarly. They did so to the point of putting it on a cross. It died with its head to one side, its eyes turned back, like a simple bird nailed to a wall. And it was Osiris, Isis, Brahma, Vishnu, Apollo, Zeus, Iaveh—all of them, all of them! All of them died on the gibbet of the Christ!"

A kind of brief sob upset her mask and twisted her lips momentarily.

"They're dead! They're dead!"

For a moment she directed her pupils toward something invisible, then gradually calmed down, and, lowering her voice, went on solemnly:

"They died of having become palpable, measurable and ponderable, in the person of Jesus. For the living are unworthy to touch the divinity. It is said in the first chapter and the first sentence of the Tao Te Ching: 'The

---

1 *Rabb* is an Arabic word meaning lord or master.

name that can be named is not the eternal name.' And the Jews also knew that, who dared not pronounce the name of Iaveh and called him, trembling, Adonai. But since someone was able to put his fingers in the wounds of the Incarnate, never again will peoples prostrate themselves before the unknowable. And now the human vermin have invaded the forbidden vault and are swarming at their ease in the beard of the Eternal."

Lower still, she articulated: "Everything is consummated!"

Then she fell silent.

Mutely, they watched the fixed smile that lingered on her lips for a long time. Finally, she passed her hands over her eyes, appeared to wake up from a hypnosis, and murmured:

"It's necessary to try hard to console ourselves. The gospels are the supreme crash of the divine, but the people, with their instinct, have saved something from the bankruptcy: the cathedrals, the stained glass windows, the incense, the legends and the superstitions still remain to us. But how long can we live on that debris? Afterwards, there will only be *Ecce homo*, alas!"

And suddenly, in her most imperative voice, she ordered: "Let's work!"

Half of the month of January went by in the fever of work. The classification of the inestimable documents of Elephantine was reaching its end. The princess went as far as to give Charles-Étienne permission to photograph as he wished the furniture, the objects, the jewels, including the great Hathor with a cow's head, and even the demotic writings and the hieroglyphs in the crypt.

Agitated by the exaltations of the day, the young man began to lose sleep. How many nights he had the desire to get up from his bed, as vast as a mausoleum, to return to his dear table, where the book was being elaborated! But he did not want to work without Geneviève. And would it not be betraying the princess to continue to study and comment on her riches without her?

Lying under the sheets, his pajamas open, his hair gracefully disordered, he strove to close his eyes and to go to sleep to the monotonous rumble of the cataract. Sometimes he switched on the light again and smoked a cigarette.

Alone in the silence of the dormant palace, he thought bitterly about the happiness of being young and loving as he had loved since childhood. Imminent glory sang within him, a magnificent recompense for his effort, and that glory was the booty that he would bring to Geneviève, by virtue of which he would merit that she would finally be entirely his. Once, as an idle child, in order to see her smile, he had obtained the prize of honor. Now, in order for her to become his wife, he needed renown and money. A joyful intoxication possessed him. He was glad not to find sleep, and to be able to think about her with that tremulous fervor, while she was asleep at the other end of the palace, without knowing that he was awake, prey to his incalculable amour.

He wondered what his youth would have been if, in the humble church of Bellecour, when he was eight years old, a little queen of France had not appeared to him, emerging for him from the four colors of the stained glass window, to the ineffable sounds of a Bach prelude. The heart of a man had been born then in the breast of a child, a precocious flower, and his entire life had been orientated at that moment.

Egyptology came to me from her, and then Egypt. It's because of her and for her that I'm here, in Elephantine— me, little Misserand, a duffer destined to advance to mediocrity under all its forms. It's because of her and for her that I shall be rich and famous. Everything by means of her and for her, and nothing without her. I love her. I loved her already, as strongly as today, when I performed tumbles in the grass to make her laugh. I shall love her even more strongly when we are two old people who never quit one another, when our children will be young people in their turn, directed toward the future. Oh, when we're rich, it will be necessary for someone to sell us Bellecour farm, in order that we can spend the summers there as a family. How beautiful it will be to resume childhood where we left it in the person of our sons and daughters! I want one of them to be a musician and to play the Bach prelude that gave me my soul on Sundays at high mass. And Sainte Radegonde will smile, the transparent grandmother of our children.

Thus he was dreaming one night, to the rhythm of the first eddies of the upper Nile, when he was abruptly woken up from his dreams.

Someone—there was no doubt about it—had just entered his apartment,

Throwing away his cigarette, he leapt to his feet.

Genevieve is ill!

The door toward which he ran opened.

Princess Antinides was before him.

✳

He had the clear sensation that she had come to him at that undue hour to announce a misfortune.

"Geneviève?" he cried, in a hoarse voice.

Still in black against the obscure background of the doorway, only the face of Antigone emerged from the drapes of her light robe and the nocturnal shadows. A pallor of the tomb made her eyes even larger than usual.

"Geneviève is asleep," she murmured. "Everyone is asleep. Don't worry, nothing has happened

He breathed out forcefully.

"Oh, I was afraid!" he murmured, disconcerted

And immediately, his face expressed: *Then what are you doing here?*

With an embarrassed gesture, his hands adjusted the open neck of his pajamas and sought to smooth the tumultuous wisps of his hair, full of blond gleams.

"From where I am," she said, without appearing to notice his embarrassment, "and as I don't sleep, I can hear the slightest sound that is produced in the palace. You've marched back and forth, you've opened a window . . . and then, I've seen your light. So, you're like me . . . you don't sleep. Then why not profit from your wakefulness to work? I've been thinking about it for several nights."

"Work without Geneviève?" he said, sketching a movement of recoil.

"Genevieve is delicate. We're not going to wake her at this hour, I imagine?"

He looked at her, without seeking to hide his astonishment. All the anxieties that the woman had already provoked in his mind and Geneviève's awoke again at the same time. Was this a new whim? What did she want with him? One particularly grave suspicion crossed his mind.

"Madame . . ." he stammered

"Listen! There's no point in seeking preambles. I have a secret to reveal to you—to you alone. This is the unique moment when we will be without witnesses. That's all."

"Geneviève isn't a witness!" he protested, shivering. "Geneviève is myself, and . . ."

"No."

"Please forgive me, Madame. I . . ."

"Don't continue. I believe that I can ask you one little thing, my child, in exchange for . . . my welcome at Elephantine? What do you say?"

He blushed, ashamed because of the soft voice, almost humble, that she had adopted.

"Oh, Madame!"

She considered him in his charming confusion.

"Have no fear. This secret is another thing that will aid you in your work. It's a matter of a new crypt," she continued, very rapidly. "I prefer to tell you about it immediately. But this one is so sacred that it requires universal slumber for me to dare to talk about it. Come, come with me! It's tonight that I shall enable you to penetrate it." And as he remained motionless and chilled: "We can only go there by night, because no one should even see which way we are heading. And apart from the fact that it's necessary not to fatigue Geneviève, she would be too impressed by what we are going to visit."

Her voice resumed more slowly in order to articulate almost in a whisper: "We're going among the dead."

A panic fear abruptly took possession of Charles-Étienne. He was alone in the night in confrontation with a madwoman.

She did not take her eyes off him. With an increasing terror, he wanted to turn his head away, to flee, and to lock himself in his room. Too late. With the jerky gait of a somnambulist, he began to walk, and when she opened the door again, he began to follow her in spite of himself.

XIII

L ATER, he was to write:
I was unaware at that time of the theatrical disposition of certain modern Muslim sepulchers, hidden
flagstones lifted up by means of a ring and descents underground to reach the realm of the dead. Once again,
the sentiment of a deceptive stage set crossed my mind.

After having crossed the whole of the nocturnal garden stealthily, we reached a kind of crossroads between
the palm trees. There stood a small but massive round
stone building, a construction devoid of an opening that
I had previously assumed to be an Arab mausoleum.

My guide had stopped dead. I saw her, by the confused light of a quarter moon, moving thick sand away
from the base. As everything had been incomprehensible
for me since her appearance in my room, I simply waited
for some new manifestation of her bizarrerie.

After ten minutes of her clearance, the disengaged
base of the building allowed its secret to appear. The wall
could be opened. In the savant hands of the princess,
it suddenly appeared to be entirely unsealed. Through
the narrow gap thus contrived we penetrated into the
interior.

The fissure closed upon us smoothly. We were in the obscurity of a tomb. The princess took the small lamp with which I was familiar from her black garments. There was nothing inside the building but empty space.

She leaned over one of the flagstones in the floor and opened it by means of the same magic. The entrance to a dark stairway appeared. Antigone went down the first steps, making a sign to me to follow her.

I obeyed. In addition to the magnetic force that attached me to her footsteps, since we had set forth an almost mocking curiosity impelled me to see how far the morbid fantasy of that neurasthenic would go, whose imagination, served by billions, had no reason to know limits.

The descent of the mysterious steps took a long time. The stone stairway turned incessantly in a complicated spiral, coming to dead ends in which Antigone found a low hidden door that she alone, evidently, knew how to open.

The last door, reached after half an hour in the maze, was made of bronze, eroded by time, so much lower than the others that we had to crawl through it on our knees. I was doing my best, now, to conserve my sang-froid, but a horrible sensation gripped my heart increasingly as we went deeper underground. I knew that it would not be possible for me to get out of the maelstrom of subterranean stone into which I had been led. All the doors had closed behind us, one by one. Even with the light I would not have been able to find them again on my own and even having found them, I would not have known the secret of their closures.

It was, in fact, better, I said to myself, that Geneviève had not accompanied us. I was so far away from her now, so perfectly lost, so completely delivered to the woman who was preceding me, that the bleak sentiment of my impotence was beginning to drain all my courage away. The mockery disappeared from my mind to give way to that certainty.

Having stood up again after crawling on my knees, I was standing beside the princess in the center of a classic hypogeum—but an intact hypogeum.

The first crypt shown a few weeks earlier greatly reduced the astonishment that this one might have caused me. I had expected the worst, and in sum, found myself once again in a museum atmosphere, a continuation of marvels already delivered to my ardent investigation by the generosity of our hostess.

A rather singular thing: finding myself, in the very heart of darkness, in the midst of those rows of sarcophagi, drew a sigh of relief from my breast. At the point where I was, after that disquieting descent into the entrails of the ground, I said to myself: *It's nothing but this!*

A smile of deliverance must have appeared on my face when I exclaimed: "What splendor!"

But the solemn gesture of the princess and the expression on her face plunged me back into a problematic state of mind when she presented the sarcophagi to me with the two words: "My family!"

She did not leave me the time for an exclamation. Her lamp was already illuminating at close range the first of the funereal inscriptions. In a loud voice she read the formulae, with so much ease, and so quickly, that it was impossible for me mentally to translate a single word. Drawing nearer, I leaned over in order to spell out awkwardly and try to understand in my turn the meaning of the characters, but she was already going toward the second sarcophagus, depriving me of the light in order to illuminate the new inscriptions. She read them in equal haste, with the guttural inflections that I had noticed the first time she had begun to decipher the stones before Genevieve and me.

After the third inscription she stopped. "And so on . . ." she murmured.

I saw her direct the luminous beam of her lamp toward the depths of the mortuary chamber. A gleam lit up in the shadow of a recess. A very narrow golden door was revealed. What other mystery was about to open?

Suddenly turning toward me, the princess showed me one of those previously-encountered gazes that had made me shudder every time. Almost in a whisper she proffered: "This is the secret of secrets."

She took one more step, put her eyes very close to mine, and concluded, through clenched teeth: "But you'll only know it if you merit it."

She addressed me as *tu*, at which I recoiled without her seeming to perceive it. Her dancing steps were already heading for the door by which we had entered.

"Let's go back up!" she said.

Without daring to insist on making a closer study of the formidable chamber of the dead revealed by her caprice, I followed her, glad to see our anguishing expedition coming to an end. But I took account of the fact that, after climbing twenty steps, she engaged in a new spiral of the subterranean palace, and soon, the new door that she opened allowed us to penetrate into a vast room with marble walls, surrounded by marble benches, the accumulated carpets of which were soft underfoot.

"This is the chamber in which the living come to keep company with the dead," she declared, on the threshold.

Almost supernatural in her black garments in the midst of such décor, it was in a perfectly natural voice that she explained: "The modern Egyptians still practice that rite in the great Islamic families . . . but without knowing why. As here, they have the catafalque in the middle of the chamber"—the catafalque was, in fact, there—"but they deposit a Koran there, of which each visitor must read a few lines on entering."

Her finger pointed toward the carpet on which we were walking. "The sarcophagi are directly below."

She aimed the beam of her projector. "In that niche, those jars, goblets, baskets of fruits and cakes are what they eat and drink while chatting. That also has been perpetuated in our day by the local pachas and princes. To keep company with the dead, is to live among them, isn't it?"

The tone that she adopted would have been reassuring in any other circumstances. However, while my intrigued eyes kept watch on her gestures, I could not bring myself to pronounce a single word.

Finally, she put down her lamp in such a fashion as to illuminate us comfortably. I saw her take from the niche and deposit on a low table—archaic, like everything else—two goblets, a jar, and three baskets of fruits and cakes. And while making those preparations with a tranquility more stupefying than the rest, she told me: "I often come here alone. For example, on the days when you didn't see me, I was here. I also come on the nights when I can't sleep..."

She also said: "This catafalque is above a certain sarcophagus..."

A hermetic smile concluded the statement

I did not miss a single one of her movements. She seemed satisfied with the disposition of her table.

"Now," she said, "We're going to keep the dead company."

Why did she put her fingers on the catafalque? Covered with ancient golden cloth, it appeared, when she parted the folds, to be made of a light and precious wood, a frail carcass artfully wrought by hands thousands of years ago, without a doubt.

"I fabricated it myself," she announced to me, however. "One of my husbands was a carpenter and had taught me to work in wood. For no one around me knows of the existence of this chamber, or that of the hypogeum."

With that, with a rapid sweep of the hand, she made the lid of the catafalque swivel on hinges, uncovering a kind of bed covered with cushions and colored blankets. Supply, she lay down among them. Her arm extended to invite me.

"Come and lie down next to me and eat," she said, in a coaxing voice that I had never heard before.

A new transformation of her changing physiognomy suddenly showed me a woman that I had not so far suspected in the somber and desperate Antigone. Her almost-closed eyes only allowed a line of black light to filter between the joined lashes; her nostrils were opening and closing rapidly; her sensually taut mouth showed the dazzling teeth; and the panting of her breast lifted up the black fabric in accordance with the same rhythm that caused the wings of her nose to beat.

A gesture of calculated slowness parted the black cloth while the bare feet kicked off the little modern shoes that sheathed them, one after the other. Her nudity appeared in a kind of golden net, an amber siren whose breasts terminated in two somber dots. I had before me, alive, one of the pharaonnes whose little statues, in museums, have shoulders much broader than the hips, long legs and a narrow round neck like a tower.

"Come!" she murmured.

I clenched my jaws. The scene that I had been expecting obscurely since she had come into my room had finally been produced. My suspicions confirmed, the disturbance that rose within me, the astonishment, the scandal and the peremptory assurance that the more than enigmatic woman really was the dangerous creature foreseen since the first glance in Paris, that whole flood of sensations and thoughts was summarized in a single clamor:

"It isn't you that I love!"

The growl with which she responded to me seemed the natural cry of the wild beast that she suddenly became. Her gaze became darker. Emerging completely from her mourning dress, on her knees on the bed, she opened her arms, twisting them like gilded serpents. Her chin advanced, she tilted back her face among the short blue curls of her hair; and, her lips parted, she offered her crimson mouth, all the way to the depths of her throat.

"Geneviève!" I repeated. "Geneviève!"

The seductress got to her feet, walked toward me, and surrounded me with all her being. She appealed to my male brutality. It was brutally that I pushed her away.

"It's Geneviève that I love! I can't and never will be able to love anyone but her!"

I was finally able to disengage the hands that were trying to draw me away. The body that was stuck to mine, violently rejected, fell back upon the bed, and straightened up there with a bound. Sitting in the middle of the cushions, Antigone gazed at me, shaken by a sob devoid of tears.

"Oh, why isn't it me that you love" she pronounced, dully. Her shoulders raised, her fists at her cheeks, she continued passionately: "You who know how to love, the only one who knows how to love . . ."

Her arms were imploring.

"I love you! If you suspected that prodigy! Oh, love me, love me! I'll give you everything that I am, everything that I have, everything that I know. You'll be the king of the world. And me . . . your love would save me. If you knew . . . !"

With a nervous hand she struck the bed.

"Do you know what there is down there, a few meters away? My deliverance, alas! My deliverance . . . !

"What are you saying?" I cried. "Can't you see that I've had enough of your puzzles, finally?"

A wave of anger and scorn lifted me up. The carnal desire that she was trying to provoke in me was transposed into hatred in my taut nerves. My desire was to beat that excessively beautiful queen who was offering herself with the magnificent indecency of a beast. For that insult made to Geneviève, to the amour I had for Geneviève, to our dream, to our childhood, I felt capable of punishing her by death.

She understood very well what was happening within me, for a smile stranger than all the others appeared on her dolorous face.

"Yes," she murmured, "yes . . . if you could kill me . . . ?"

More provocative, more tremulous, she was against me again. The warmth of her body caught in the golden mesh, her precious, as if archaic, beauty, her intoxicating perfume, those nacreous eyes, the mouth that she was opening for me, multiplied tenfold the disgust she inspired in my mind, precisely because of the temptation of my flesh.

"You, who are so pure," she moaned, "you who have only ever loved one woman, a woman who is not yet yours . . ."

Why did the wretched woman dare to evoke Geneviève? The fashion in which I seized her wrists in order to tear her way from me for a second time must have left bruises on her delicate skin. Our struggle was mute and long. In the end, having retreated into a corner, I looked at her from a distance, arms folded in the attitude of the most glacial disdain

Curled up amid the disorder of the bed into which she had just fallen again, I saw a human panther ready for a prodigious bound.

A silence of a few seconds preceded her attack. My heart was hammering. I had the certainty that, one way or another, I would not emerge alive from that scene, which made her my implacable enemy.

I waited, ready to die for my sole amour.

But the bound was not produced. Suddenly standing up, calm and cold, she slowly put on her mantle of black pleats again, enclosing herself within it without haste, went to the lamp and, over her shoulder, with all the dignity of a sovereign, darted at me like an order:

"Let's go! We'll return to the palace now."

Hallucinated by what I had just lived, alone again in my room, I tried throughout the rest of the night to reflect on the situation. And in the semi-darkness full of the noise of the Nile, I sensed my dilated eyes becoming ever wider.

XIV

THE next morning, as soon as Genevieve had got up, he went to knock on her door.

Without saying bonjour to her, unkempt, his pajamas ragged, he said: "We need to get away from here, Geneviève. Let's go, quickly!"

She thought he was mad.

"What's the matter with you?" she asked, gently.

He almost stammered: "The princess came to my room last night, and I understood that she was insane. She's in full crisis. I'm afraid of her. I'm afraid for you, and for myself. Quickly, quickly, let's return to Paris!"

"My poor Charlet . . ." murmured the young woman, calmly. She examined him, smiling, and went on: "Come and sit down here. Tell me about it."

But instead of being appeased, as usual, by his fiancée's sang-froid, little Masserand made a violent gesture. The terrors and brutalities of the night were still in his distraught features.

"I tell you that it's necessary to leave this very day!"

"Come on, Charlet," she recommenced. "Come and sit down, and tell me . . ."

He interrupted her, speaking at the same time as her. "Let's go! Let's go! Let's get out!"

"But what is it that can possibly have put you in such a state?"

He opened his mouth, but said nothing. He could not take it upon himself to tell Geneviève the truth.

"I'll tell you later!" he murmured

She was astonished, but did not let him see it. Without persisting, for the moment, in trying to discover the secret, the first one he had not confided to her, she said, composedly: "I can see that something grave has happened. But how do you expect to get out of here without the princess knowing? We're her prisoners, after all."

The young man looked at her, petrified. Panic made him tremble. Geneviève was about to speak again, when the princess came in, as she did every day at that time.

On seeing her, Charles-Étienne became livid. Without waiting, he rushed forward, saying no matter what.

"Madame, we must leave immediately. We've just received a telegram."

She gazed at him profoundly. She knew full well that it was not true. Without even taking the trouble to pretend to be surprised, she smiled, almost amused.

"Poor children!" she said. "Well, the auto is at your disposal to take you to Alexandria, if you wish."

Geneviève lowered her head. That attitude, even more than Charlet's agitation, demonstrated to her that something definitive had, indeed, happened while she was sleeping tranquilly during the night. Entirely discountenanced, Charles-Étienne paced back and forth, his hands in the pockets of his pajamas.

"Have you at least what you need for the boat?" asked Antigone, in a low voice.

"Yes!" cried, Charles-Étienne wildly, turning his head away. "And for the train too."

Maternally, she enveloped them with her tranquil gaze. Her self-control was exasperating. "That's all right, then. I'll give orders for you to be taken to the railway station."

Noble and upright, she went out without another word, and without turning round. Geneviève was a little pale; the other clenched his fists

"Do we have enough money between us?" he wondered, nervously. "We'll need quite a lot: the tips, the train, the post office. Let's not forget the telegram for Papa. I'll help you to pack the trunks right away. Oh, I'd like to be at sea already! As long as nothing happens between now and then! As long as we have enough money!"

A sad aftermath of the splendors in which they had gorged themselves for so many days, they returned on the steamer in steerage, prey to seasickness. They had not seen the princess again. All the tips offered had been refused, fortunately for them, for their money was only just sufficient to take them back, without a sou to spare, even for their nourishment.

※

When the initial effusions had passed, Jean Masserand said: "Now that you've recovered, will you explain to us the faces that you have?"

"After your enthusiastic letters!" Monsieur de Belle-cour added

Charles-Étienne finally confessed: "Princess Antinides is half mad. We were afraid of her and we came back."

"Ah!" exclaimed the Academician.

Sitting on the old sofa in his study between his son and his future daughter-in-law, he took them by the hands with a great emotion.

"I daren't write to you for fear of chilling your enthusiasm and compromising your book, but—Bellecour knows what I'm talking about—that woman, in sum, is simply an adventuress. I'll tell you everything now."

His pretty blue eyes caressed the two expectant children by turns.

"My dears, this is what has happened. A week after your departure, old Chables came to see me in a state of extraordinary excitement. Perhaps he's a little mad himself . . . he's so old! You remember his faint at the end of the famous soirée? He said to me: 'Fool! You've let them depart on the yacht of that Antinides? Do you know why I fell unconscious that evening? Frightened by her exact resemblance to Belkis Effendi, a wretch who doomed me in my youth, I had asked her whether she was not her granddaughter or great-granddaughter. She had just replied to me, impudently, that she was not, that Belkis was a Turkish name and that there was nothing Turkish about her. Just at that moment, lowering my eyes, I saw the ring that she was wearing on her finger: a large gold ring…'"

"Yes! Yes!" said the two fiancés in unison, gripped.

"Oh, you know it, that ring?" continued the Academician. "Good! Listen carefully, then. Old Chables, strangled by emotion, told me this: that same ring, the Belkis of his youth wore on her finger. She had been the duc's mistress for a long time. One day, he perceived that he was deceived. That was the great drama of the poor old man's life. He was madly in love with that Turk run aground in Paris. She had already ruined him; now she was making a fool of him. After a duel, and after all the scenes that you can imagine, he returned to her house one day to beg her to have pity on him and to let him back into her life. When she rejected him cruelly he threw himself on his knees. Then she struck him in the face, and the ring wounded him in the temple." Jean Masserand finished in a lower voice: "He parted his white hair in order to show me the scar…"

A silence followed that, while the siren of a boat screeched on the Seine. Uncle de Bellecour shook his head. Jean Masserand looked at the fiancés in order to see their impression, but neither of them gave it to him.

"Nothing astonishes me…" said Charles-Étienne, in a low voice. And that was all.

"Perhaps I was mistaken not to tell you that story right away?" asked the father anxiously. "To begin with, it was difficult to write that to you. One never knows the true fate of a letter. And then, I repeat, you were so intoxicated by joy and work that I was afraid. Finally, after obtaining such precise information from Taillefer

. . . can one know how far the imagination of an old fossil like the Duc de Chables might go? You're not saying anything . . . was I wrong or not?"

But they did not reply to that question.

As energetic as ever, Geneviève had reorganized the work without delay.

Sitting at their table, the Egyptian parenthesis closed, they resumed life where they had left it. Bleak and sage, they only spoke to one another in monosyllables, in accordance with the necessities of the labor. The silence they maintained, even between themselves, regarding the adventure in Elephantine, loomed up on either side of the table like an invisible wall.

An embarrassment remained to them because of the secret that Charles-Étienne did not reveal. That malaise was added to the cold of winter in Paris, to the grayness of Paris and the paltriness of life in Paris, as many habitudes difficult to resume now that they had known the sumptuousness and light of the Antinides palace.

Poring over their poor work, they worked without enthusiasm. Everything was now lacking. Without the atmosphere of Egypt, without the treasures in the midst of which they had lived in phantasmagoria and ardor, without the documents delivered in profusion to their avidity, without the princess to guide them, they sensed that their dear book would no longer be anything but an abortive work.

One morning, unable to support that life any longer, Charles-Étienne suddenly burst into sobs

Very straight, with her eyebrows furrowed, Geneviève touched him on the shoulder.

"Come on, Charlet. Tell me, now. It will be better for both of us."

Did she believe him to be culpable? He shuddered at that idea. She had certainly divined something of the truth. Perhaps she was blaming him. Since childhood, absolute and inflexible, she had been ready not to love him any longer, he knew, if he had broken the tacit, mystical pact that attached them to one another.

The horror that traversed his soul at that idea reckoned with the modesty of sorts that had retained him this far. Honest and tremulous, he recounted in every detail the subterranean scene at Elephantine. She could not disbelieve what he said. The slightest doubt would have been a crime for her.

She advanced toward him when he had finished.

"How you love me," she murmured. And for the first time, he saw the gaze of a woman pass through her icy eyes.

She had leaned over. They exchanged their first amorous kiss.

Now, life had rediscovered its light. The work was done with more joy, the mist of the Occidental winter appeared less dense.

In spite of their frequent sessions with the Egyptian antiquities of the Louvre, however, the two young people increasingly lost the golden thread that had guided them during the days in Elephantine.

They made superhuman efforts to reconstitute from memory the unusual documentation they had had in their hands during their dream-like sojourn, but the notes made in the Antinides palace could not replace the photographs that they had not had time to take, and in any case, more weeks in Egypt would have been necessary merely to complete the plan of their work such as they had modified it on the spot. The prey having escaped, nothing remained to them but the shadow. Instead of the sensational book that ought to have enabled them to enter into life with a splash, it was necessary to resign themselves to falling back into reality. Their contribution to Egyptology would simply be that on which they had counted before the voyage: an honorable volume whose sales would doubtless permit them finally to marry and to live very modestly on their first work while waiting for another to follow.

Courageous but disappointed, they accepted that destiny. Their amour was there, more intense than ever, to heal the wounds of the fall.

XV

THE glimmer of femininity that he had seen in Geneviève's eyes was not renewed. The fascinating coldness of that young creature, and her ever-impenetrable mystery, continued to exercise their emprise on the former small boy of Beautilleul.

She had said: "It's necessary that your book will be a success even so, and we'll arrive at that!"

Then he believed her, and hope returned from day to day.

A little fever began to beat again in his blood. Since Geneviève still had faith, nothing, in sum, was lost for him. The idea that finishing the book would announce the preparations for their marriage reinflated the courage that he had lost so completely at first.

Spring was about to be established in the clearer air, the days were getting longer, the age-old miracle that gives leaves again to dead trees was beginning to work upon the branches hanging over the quays of the Seine.

One morning, as the fiancés sat down bravely at their table in spite of the malaise of sorts that the end of March brings to people, at the same time, undoubtedly, as to trees on the way to becoming green again, as they strove to forget their youth in order to absorb themselves in their arid daily work, a considerable package arrived in the post along with a few letters. It was addressed to *Monsieur Charles-Étienne Masserand*, but in parentheses the mention was inscribed: *and Geneviève*. It came from Egypt; the handwriting was unknown.

"What can this be?" Charles-Étienne exclaimed, intrigued.

"Open it," said Geneviève, serenely. "That's the only means of knowing."

Feverishly, the young man cut the wrapping, removing the superimposed layers of paper one by one. Large photographs finally appeared between two sheets of cardboard.

"Oh!" cried Charles-Étienne.

His hand trembled as he handed the first of the images to Geneviève. The princes had sent them admirable portraits of all the furniture, objects, statues and inscriptions in the crypt of Elephantine. Pinned to the last photograph was a letter:

Forgive a poor desperate woman sometimes ready to lose her reason. You have sometimes been able to take account of my condition. I do not know myself how far I will go in those fatal crises, but I have been having treatment since your departure. You can see that I am perfectly cured, since I have been able to take pictures of the entire collection that you have seen, by means of magnesium. May I be useful to you thus. You will find a few papyri, the most essential, in the box that is adjoining to this. Don't judge me without

appeal. The shame of my last divagations has been an un-
speakable suffering to me, in which I think I have exhausted
all the dolor of this world.

Charles-Étienne's intonation was that of a ten-year-old child: "All the same!"

Angry, certainly, but glad in spite of himself, it was while quivering that he opened the precious box of ancient wood and touched the fragile papyri. All the notes that they had made, which had remained unusable, rediscovered their passionate interest, thanks to those photographs, and thanks to those inestimable writings.

He raised his eyes to look at Geneviève and to discover what she thought.

Scorn, gratitude and commiseration were evident in the voice of the young woman when she murmured, with a slight shrug of the shoulders: "Poor woman!"

The present was accepted. Charles-Étienne respired profoundly.

"We can also take advantage of it to thank her for her hospitality," said the young woman. "We left without even saluting her, after all that she had done for us. That's scarcely decent, it seems to me."

There was no rancor in her noble heart.

"We'll do as you wish," said Charles-Étienne, with a fearful expression.

And from that moment on, they only thought, joyfully, about gazing at and touching their treasure.

✳

Once again, the book was orientated in a sensational direction. All sorts of furniture, objects, sacred vases, lamps, ex-votos and musical instruments, of which no one had yet seen the models in museums, would illustrate Charles-Étienne's pages. To describe them without showing the reproductions would have been folly. In the matter of documentation, what is not proven is charged with imposture. Similarly, the inscriptions in stone and the characters of papyrus figured in the work. What emotion young Masserand's commentary supporting such images, explaining them as the princess had explained each of the unknown marvels of her crypt, would cause in the scholarly world!

"Oh, what a pity it is that she's no longer here to finish enlightening us!" sighed Charles-Étienne. "So many things remain about which she hadn't said anything."

"Yes . . ." replied Geneviève, thoughtfully.

They kept their work absolutely secret. Even Jean Masserand was excluded from their mysterious book. They did not want to show anyone the photographs, and did not want anyone apart from themselves to know of their existence. The problem was having them reproduced when the moment came.

"We'll find a means," Geneviève declared.

And because she affirmed it, Charles-Étienne was sure of it.

They had written the requisite letter to thank their benefactress. Their conscience was tranquil. With intoxication, they rediscovered, or very nearly, the great excitement of Elephantine.

She did not give them any warning. One morning in May, she simply sent them her card.

"This lady is at the entrance," said the housekeeper, innocently

Charles-Étienne had leapt to his feet, distressed. Even Geneviève uttered a slight cry.

"Her!"

They were immobilized momentarily, looking at one another.

Then: "Have the lady come in," said Geneviève, serenely.

She came in, dancing, smiling, elegant and modern.

"Still at work, naturally!"

In spite of her costume, labeled Rue de la Paix, all of ancient Egypt, formidable and sacred, had just entered the modest room along with her. The fiancés sensed it with an intoxication so violent that, forgetting the painful drama that had brutally separated them from her, they launched themselves forward with a unanimous impulse.

"My dear children . . ." she murmured

And that was the first time that they saw a human emotion pass through the depths of her large enameled eyes, which never looked anywhere but inwards.

※

Jean Masserand was only admitted to see her in the drawing room. He alone appeared embarrassed by her

unexpected presence. Involuntarily, his eyes went incessantly to the large gold ring.

"It's curious, isn't it?" said the princess finally. "I
found it three years ago, in London, in the establishment
of a Turkish antiquarian."

And that would have been all had the sigh of relief
uttered by all three of them not revealed the suspicion
that had weighed upon her.

Complaisantly, she held out her precious hand in
order to display the ring at closer range.

"The bezel ought to open up," she continued, "but
I've never found the secret of it. It is, however, a ring of
great value. Pure primitive Egyptian—have you seen it,
Charles-Étienne? The old Turk never had any idea what
he was selling me."

Her sad smile passed. "Are we going to work together
again?"

It was Geneviève who hastened to respond.

"Madame," she said, "we will never be able to thank
you as much as we would like for your generosity toward
us."

"Then you're willing to take me back as a collaborator?"

"Oh! Madame . . ."

The dramatic eyes paused on Geneviève for a long
moment.

"Thank you. You know that you are saving my life . . ."

She extended her hands to Jean Masserand. "Your
children, Monsieur can tell you that they have worked a
miracle. They believe they owe me gratitude and yet, it's
me who will never be able to thank them enough. They
are giving me back an appetite for life."

A second pallor had extended over her face of white marble. For a moment, her eyes closed, she was a statue of despair. Then she shook her head, tried to smile again, and asked: "Would you like us to begin right away?"

Proudly defiant, Geneviève therefore accepted, between her and her fiancé, the continual presence of her terrible rival of one night. Did she think that, in fact, she had only acted that night in a morbid crisis, now unrenewable? Was she sure of her emprise to the point of having no fear of another, even such a dangerous other? Did she want to test the fidelity of her Tristan or, perversely, was she tempting destiny?

That secret was to remain forever hers, behind the impenetrable ice of her gray eyes, extended, under the delicate and pale eyebrows, as if by the thrust of a Medieval thumb.

XVI

M^{Y dear children,}
      It is, therefore, in a week that you will be married, and I shall not be with you . . . I would not want to sound a sad note amid your joy, but I confess to you that I bless the circumstances that have obliged me to return to Elephantine to organize my museum, now that it is to become the prey of visitors

That beautiful wedding at Beautilleul would remind me too cruelly of my lost happiness. I have already had occasion, unfortunately, to appeal to your pity, a forgotten bad dream. You have had the grandeur to pardon me for a moment of irresponsibility. It is necessary today to pardon me for a moment of lucidity.

Understand me well. I am not jealous of your happiness. Oh God, have I wished for it ardently enough? You know that I have done everything to aid you to conquer it, and how ardently I have tried to direct your work on the right path.

Charles-Étienne is now famous and rich; you have been able to buy back the house of your childhood, all the newspapers continue ardent polemics on the subject of his

Unknown Egypt *more than a year after publication. Thus, we have accomplished our desires and more. I thank the gods of Quamit,*[1] *who have certainly acted for us. But to witness your marriage would not only have been dolorous for me but dangerous.*

Any allusion to my first youth risks causing me to fall back into those temporary derangements of which you have seen a few fatal specimens. In the midst of work, with both of you by my side, I certainly sense that I am cured of all my nervous troubles, but an atmosphere of condensed celebration around two young heads is not at all what I need. I could not be other than tragic in the midst of the general pleasure, and I would appear, with my type already so affirmed, a bird of ill omen fallen into the joy of others.

No, my presence at your marriage is unnecessary. From afar, I shall think of you; I shall send you all my fluids, and all my prayers to the divinities of the earth. You will also receive, almost at the same time as this letter, a bronze miniature of my great Hathor, a statue of the same epoch, and also a few jewels from my collection for Geneviève. Those wedding presents will remind you of Elephantine, while waiting for you to return there with me one day, in accordance with your promise.

I shall also keep my promise. Once my museum is installed—oh, Charles-Étienne, what have you wrought with your book! but after all, I owe that crypt to you after having given you its fruits—I shall doubtless go to make a few small tours in Europe and, finally, if it is summer,

---

1 I have left this word as it appears in the original; it is presumably a rendering of *kmt*, sometimes rendered *kemet* or *kamt*, the ancient name of Egypt, meaning "the black land."

I shall disembark suddenly in the Beautilleul that I don't know, and about which you talked to me so pleasantly aboard the Amanit . . . *do you remember?*

At present, my dear children, I embrace you both with an equal tenderness. I am writing for you here the talisman Bah! Dah![1] *which preserves from evil. I am with you in spirit, I am your friend, forever grateful to you.*

Antigone

They only saw her again after ten months of marriage, when Geneviève was nursing her first-born.

Little Carlo did not prevent her mother from supervising the preparations that were made at Beautilleul to receive Princess Antinides, the magicienne of a touching happiness.

The two spouses, each in accordance with their temperament, put all their heart into preparing the apartment that they reserved for their magnificent friend. Charlet clapped his hands; Geneviève, her eyebrows furrowed, made sure that everything was harmonious and disposed the last bouquets in the vases

"Nothing will ever approach Elephantine," she said, "but the princess has been habituated to our manner of living for a long time and, in sum, for a country house, this one isn't too badly conditioned.

"Yes! All comfort is here, since the great works!"

---

1 Probably an attempted phonetic rendering of two Hebrew letters, found linked in the Old Testament, although their function as a talisman is dubious.

150

Charles-Étienne continued, proudly. "And then, it goes without saying that it's nice in our home!"

"Yes, Charlet . . . push off! You're getting in the way of my flower arranging."

"Good! But let me kiss you, my love!"

"What a great fool you are! After ten months! The honeymoon is officially over. Are you forgetting that you're a father of a family?"

"The honeymoon will never be over for me, Geneviève. I love you."

"I've known that for a long time!"

"Yes, since I was eight years old . . ."

"Come on, Charlet, enough! Be reasonable. We have our entire lives ahead of us . . ."

"Oh, my beloved iceberg, an entire life isn't enough . . . your dear eyes full of things . . . do you know that you still intimidate me? How can I explain it to you? Under your gaze, one always has the impression of being an inferior or a rascal."

"Yes! Look out—here comes the maid . . ."

They had both wanted to wait at the gate that now closed the hedges. While watching the bend where the limousine would appear, they regretted together that the Château de Bellecour was now a sanitarium.

"She could have bought it! We could have seen her more frequently." After all the phases of their intimacy with her, they loved her definitively. Apart from the fact that it was a matter of a great duty, because of what she had given them, it was henceforth also a great sentiment in their hearts. That panther, which sometimes roared so terribly, was domesticated for them and they no longer knew anything but her material purr. They avoided talking, or even thinking, about some of her aberrations, in order no longer to see anything in her but their marvelous protectress. They would have liked her, if not to be happy, at least to be delivered from the blackest of her eternal mourning, and, in an absolutely sure fashion, also liberated from her returns of folly, for which they pitied her, with frissons of horror.

"There she is!"

The cloud of dust stopped in its course. The door of the vehicle opened.

"My children!"

They were in her arms, both talking at the same time, ecstatic at seeing her again, so beautiful, so young, and so fresh in her pallor in spite of the fatigue of the journey.

"And Carlo?" she asked, immediately. Linking arms, the three of them advanced lightly toward the house.

"Geneviève has filled out!" she said, after greeting Jean Masserand and Uncle de Bellecour. A hint of disapproval in her voice implied that she was thinking *fatter and uglier*, but she refrained carefully from saying so.

"That's what always happens when breast-feeding," replied Charles-Étienne, with a tender gaze for his wife.

And as the nurse appeared with the child, there were no more words for anything except little Carlo, already very similar to his mother.

That first day could not terminate without a pilgrimage to the memories of the two young spouses. It was Antigone who requested it, as soon as tea had been taken.

The month of August, its thick verdure, its Prussian blue shadows and its great azure free of cloud, recomposed with the exactitude of a mirror, the décor of the childhood days of Charlet and Geneviève. The presence of someone for whom they were doing the honors of the past for the first time gave the memories a strangely new luster. When, in the wind of a new auto, on the eve of their marriage, the fiancés had toured their childhood, they had not had the emotion that came to them today, while they explained their sentimental landscapes to the princess.

"There's the great lawn along which Geneviève composed the daisy-chain ..." On the way they had recounted all the petty events of those puerile days. The directors of the sanitarium allowed them circulate freely in the park.

"It's here that Geneviève showed me the crescent moon like a ring on her finger ..."

"It's this fir tree that Charlet climbed on the day he broke his leg ..."

"This is the pathway where we ran so fast ..."

Gravely, Antigone registered everything with her fatal expression.

"Now," she said, finally, "show me the window under which Charles-Étienne saw Geneviève for the first time ..."

The story of the window had not been recounted in its entirety. Of that sacred episode of their life, the point of departure for their amour, they dared not reveal the secret even to the princess. In the silent and empty little church, they remained mute regarding the beautiful fairy tale.

"It's thirteenth-century," said Geneviève, simply. "Isn't it beautiful?"

"Very beautiful . . ." replied Antigone, without overmuch enthusiasm.

To their surprise, she climbed up on one of the rear benches in order to examine the glasswork at closer rage; she seemed to make a host of reflections, and got down again without communicating any of them. Afterwards she retreated in the nave in order to appreciate the ensemble, and suddenly exclaimed: "But one might think that Sainte Radegonde was Geneviève!"

They shuddered, without knowing why

"Don't you think so?" she insisted. "One might think it was her portrait in painted glass!"

Charlet opened his mouth, smiling, in order finally to tell the story. Geneviève cut him off. Her eyes narrowing, she shook her head.

"Yes," she said, "perhaps there is something . . ."

Her husband looked at her, surprised. Why that feint? But she had her reasons, evidently. A moment passed, mysteriously, between the three. When they went through the porch again, to continue their walk, Charles-Étienne, his eyelids lowered, had the sentiment that, for the second time, he had just communed with the unknown in that church.

"Geneviève . . ." he pronounced, mentally.

And in the utmost depths of his heart, as when he was eight years old, he adored in silence the person who, secretive, disdainful and gentle, had captured his life forever.

✳

The time that the princess wanted to spend at Beautil-leul—two weeks—went by without incident, in the peace of the rustic house and that of the deserted surroundings.

Leaning over little Carlo, curious about his slightest gestures, Antigone loved to watch him being bathed, to rock him in her arms and hold him against her as he slept. When he was at the breast she remained sitting close to Geneviève and talking to her at length.

Charles-Étienne proposed excursions by auto, fishing trips, and talked about hiring horses in order to gallop over the meadows.

"No, my children. My sole pleasure is to respire your daily routine. If I could, I'd make myself invisible in order to be better able to watch you live. You're happy . . . let me contemplate my work."

"When I think," Jean Masserand never ceased repeating, "that such a simple and good woman could be treated as an adventuress by that old imbecile Chables!"

"At his age, it's permissible to go astray," conceded Uncle de Bellecour.

Sometimes, Antigone went alone into the enlarged garden, which had become almost as vast as a park. A residue of anxiety then forced Charlet and Geneviève to set forth after an hour to look for her. They found her sitting on the grass, her face toward the sky, and they watched her almost anguishing immobility from a distance for some time before approaching her.

She did not even start on seeing them surge forth. She responded to their interrogation in advance: "No

. . . I wasn't thinking about anything. Or rather, I was thinking about everything. I was in the solar system . . ."

At other times, she said: "I thought I was a rose, the rose one sometimes becomes when one has been dead and buried for a long time."

Then, as in the time at Elephantine, the young people jogged one another imperceptibly with an elbow, which signified that when they were alone they would try to decide whether or not it was a matter of a new neurasthenic state.

One day, at table, the conversation was taken by Monsieur de Bellecour to the subject of anti-Semitism. The embarrassed expressions of Charles-Étienne and Geneviève doubtless did not escape the princess. She started to laugh: a rare thing.

"I believe that at one time, in Egypt, you thought I was Jewish," she remarked, almost gaily.

Charles-Étienne blushed. Geneviève did not flinch.

"One can know Hebrew without being of the race," she continued.

"You know Hebrew, Madame?" said the father and the uncle, in unison.

"The princess knows everything," said Geneviève, tranquilly.

A hard gaze immobilized the enamel eyes. "Everything, alas. She has spoken the truth."

The two old men exchanged a glance of amazement. Geneviève stopped them with an imperceptible sign.

"Listen," she commenced. "This morning, I believe that Carlo smiled at me. In less than two months—that's not bad, is it? We're going to try to make him do it again shortly."

XVII

MONSIEUR de Bellecour's conclusion, after the departure of the princess, was: "Delightful, charming, but slightly piqued at times. It doesn't astonish me that she frightened you in Egypt."

"Oh, in Egypt . . . !" protested Charles-Étienne. Then he shut up.

In the depths of his thought he saw again the smooth siren caught in the mesh of a laden net, her arms and mouth extended toward him while he evoked Geneviève in order to flee the nocturnal temptation.

He turned his eyes toward the latter, and understood that she had had the same thought. Their gazes penetrated one another and gave themselves to one another once again.

The life that she had led during those three weeks certainly left her with some nostalgia, for, to the surprise of the whole family, shortly after the return to Paris, at the end of October, when they believed her to be in Egypt, she appeared one morning at the door of the new apartment that Charles-Étienne and his wife now occupied in the same house.

"I'm very glad to find you," she said, without any other greeting, as she went into the vast studio. "I haven't been thinking about anything else since Beautilleul, Charlet. There's a new book to write about Egypt. Where's Geneviève?"

"First, permit me to shake your hands, my dear Madame. I can see that, after three months, you're still as well. You write so rarely, and wander so much that one is never sure on what continent you're situated."

"Bonjour, bonjour!" she said, distractedly. "I know that you're all well; I met your uncle and your father on the staircase. Geneviève isn't here?"

"Geneviève is lying down. We're all well except for her."

"What!" Antigone started.

"Oh, it's nothing serious, don't worry!" He lowered his eyes guiltily. "A new child is on the way . . ."

Antigone shook her head slowly. "What folly!" Then, very quickly: "I'd like to see her. I can't talk about new projects without her."

A slight malaise made Charles-Étienne turn his head away. Those words reminded him of others spoken by him in his room at Elephantine on a certain haunted night. He took account of the fact that the princess was observing him intently. In order to cut matters short he went swiftly toward the door.

"I'll inform Geneviève. She'll certainly receive you by her bedside."

He came back after a moment. "Come in! She'll be so happy to see you!"

Antigone did not show the effect that the bloated pallor of the young woman had on her.

"Well, Geneviève, you're not afraid that Carlo will be jealous?"

Shortly afterwards, looking at them both intently: "Before even kissing the dear little one, who, it appears, has become so handsome, this is my idea: we're going to work together again. Charlet can't stop at a single volume. It's necessary that he astonish the world again. The crypt you visited out there is exhausted, but there's another one, which your husband has seen, Geneviève."

Her voice had not hesitated over those redoubtable words. Without changing her tone she went on placidly: "It's on than crypt that we're going to work now. It will be necessary for all three of us to return to Elephantine, but in the meantime, we're going to prepare the elements of the book. That already demands a good deal of time. Are you disposed, both of you, to take up the pen again?"

As always, it was Geneviève who replied.

"Your idea is magnificent Madame. I would be so happy if Charlet resumed writing, especially with you. But for myself, I'm no longer good for anything—at least for a few months."

She sighed heavily, embarrassed by her body.

"We can't work without you," declared the princess. "We'll install ourselves in your room, won't we, Charlet?"

"No, Madame . . ." pronounced Geneviève, weakly. "I'm incapable of . . . pardon me, I think I'm going to faint . . ."

"Ah!" lamented Charles-Étienne. "This happens all the time. Hold on, my love, here are your salts. Respire! Respire!"

"Let me care for her," said Antigone.

They kept all the doors open, but the sound of their two voices barely reached Geneviève's bed.

The idea of a new book fell into their lives at the right time to put an end to certain anxieties continually repeated by the uncle and the father, who lived together now.

The sales of *Unknown Egypt* had inevitably slowed down. The lifestyle adopted since the young Egyptologist's success, the considerable expenses made at Beautilleul, two autos, one large and one small, and a new child who would augment the couple's expenses, meant that the capital so quickly amassed by Charles-Étienne was threatened with being eaten away in order to meet the expenses of such luxury.

"The second book will go even further than the first," predicted Princess Antinides—which represented henceforth the palpitating hope of the entire household.

They worked.

Once again, although he had thought that he would never be astonished again, Charles-Étienne was astounded by everything that the woman knew. She had said: "I believe that *The Secret of Egyptian Death* will be our new title. We will reconstitute all of the funeral ceremonial with details that no one suspects. We will also talk . . ."

"But how have you been able to discover all that?" he asked.

"I'll tell you one day . . . I've already promised that. In the meantime, let me speak. The things I'm telling you are authentic, believe me. I'll give you the proof when you return to Egypt."

Without looking at him, she went on: "You've only cast a glance over my hypogeum. It's full of secrets buried in hiding-places. All of my documentation is there, irrefutable."

He lowered his head a little too far over his papers, seized by shame for her at the memory of her subterrains of amour and death. How could she allude to it so calmly?

"I believe that Geneviève's calling you!" she exclaimed suddenly.

One day, when he returned after one of Geneviève's appeals:

"You don't give the impression, my child, of suspecting that she's not in a good state. Don't you see how much she has changed since you've been married?"

"Geneviève has always been very delicate."

"And you haven't been afraid for her of these successive maternities? You can see that in addition to her physical fatigue, she's excluded from the work she loved so much! At the same time as her beauty she's in the process of losing her intellectuality."

The gaze that he raised toward her was that of a believer in full ecstasy.

"Geneviève will always be the same for me," he pronounced.

And it was Princes Antinides who lowered her eyes this time before the sublime splendor of that male gaze.

The second child was expected in the middle of July. It was decided that Geneviève would give birth at Beautilleul. The specialist who was caring for her consented to that journey, affirming that everything would pass normally; he also recommended the young woman to his correspondent in the town nearest to the sanitarium of Bellecour, who was endowed with a veritable genius.

The journey was made by railway, with Geneviève lying on the banquette, her head on Antigone's knees. Facing them, the three men encouraged her with their smiles.

"I'm your maman," said the princess, "so your children are my grandchildren."

"What a young grandmother!" murmured Geneviève, trying to laugh.

"I look young, yes."

Why that drama on the jade face all of a sudden?

"You look young . . . and you are young!" remarked the invalid. "Younger than me now."

"Young, yes. Always young!"

"I can't look at you from the position I'm in, but you give the impression of blushing. There's nothing for you to lament, truly!"

"Shut up, Geneviève. How do you know that I have nothing to lament?"

There it is, thought the husband and the wife. *There's one of her whims.*

And they quickly changed the subject.

The installation in the former farm was, however, free of incident. The presence there of Antigone seemed more propitious than ever. The family did not know how to thank her for having come to assist the young mother deprived of all feminine tenderness.

The expectation of the event had interrupted the active labor of Charles-Étienne and his inspirer. Geneviève was desolate. Her great friend consoled her. She did not quit her for an instant. The first dolors saw her leaning over the bed of the courageous and writhing young woman. She spent the entire night of the birth by her bedside. It was her contralto voice that announced: "Another boy!"

There were no complications, in fact. A black nightmare drew away from the house. There was nothing more now than whiteness, an exhausted and smiling mother in immaculate sheets, a white crib next to the bed, the white comings and goings of the midwife, the physician and the nurse in a blouse, and, always leaning on the pillow, the sole dark patch, the impressive Antinides and her murmurs of felicitation.

Charles-Étienne, on his knees, kissed his wife's hands and held back the tears of a happy child.

They only recommenced occupying themselves with the book when Geneviève had recovered completely.

"We've waited for you!"

At those words, little Le Rieux shook her head.

"No, Madame, I won't work with you any more in Paris. Two children are more than enough to occupy my life now. Continue your book, the two of you, now that the fears have passed, but don't count on me to collaborate with it. One can't do everything at once. When I have the time, I'll come to sit down at your table sometimes, but that's all."

A beautiful early autumn sunset cast red patches among the displayed papers. Charles-Étienne was hurrying, before the day's end, to conclude the definitive classification of all the notes accumulated under the dictation of Antigone in eight months. The latter was reading aloud the numbers that she found as they went along on the sheets of paper on the table, the chairs and the cluttered armchairs. On his knees, he lined up on the floor the rows of files, incessantly swollen by supplementary sheets. Sitting in an armchair, Geneviève was watching them. That patient labor reminded her of the hours that she had spent herself, before her marriage, collating and classifying notes by hundreds, and heaps of paper, a frightful headache. She dared not budge for fear of disturbing her husband.

Jean Masserand came in abruptly.

"Where are you, Geneviève? It's time to bathe the children."

Behind him, the nurse was holding little Jean-Charles in her arms, and the elder, Carlo, by the hand.

Geneviève had stood up precipitately. Before any gesture could prevent him, the infant Carlo had run through the papers arranged on the floor on his unsteady legs. His father on all fours could only be a jolly game. The two little maladroit hands seized a wad to the right and one to the left. The papers flew. At the same time the child's little feet trampled joyfully amid the other piles. In a second, the disaster was accomplished.

Charles-Étienne's oath was confounded with the clamors of Geneviève, Jean Masserand and the nurse. Only the princess had remained impassive.

Geneviève had seized the child and passed him to the nurse. She looked at her husband tearing his hair.

"Three days' work!" he growled, stamping his foot. "It's too much! It's too much!"

"Perhaps I can help you," said Geneviève, softly, while the others, disappearing in haste, took the howling little criminal away.

"No!" he said, angrily. "How can you help me? You don't know the classification!"

Geneviève had already departed while he continued to exclaim.

Still red with anger, Charles-Étienne looked at the princess, in order to take her for a witness. He was struck by the expression that he thought he had surprised on her face in the fading daylight: an expression simultaneously cruel, triumphant and desperate. Under the glance of the young man she swiftly set her face straight.

"The saddest thing," she said, smiling, "is that it's nightfall. Nothing to do, with the electricity!"

"I know that very well!" he replied, with a residue of rage, switching on the light.

Antigone moved her head up and down. "All this is your fault!"

"What! How can you say that?"

"You wanted to be the father of a family; this is the result. Genevieve worn out, thickened, physically destroyed and furthermore, incapable now of participating in your work; your interior encumbered by screaming and destructive children; peace and meditation have become impossible for you. Geneviève is no longer the companion of your intellect; she's a nurse, a children's maid. While you're preparing a book like this, they permit themselves to come and disturb you, looking for her because it's time to bathe the children. You've seen how she went out to join them, without even apologizing for what has just happened. The time is not far off when she'll no longer be worthy to be your wife."

Mouth open, he contemplated her. Had he discovered something monstrous: Antigone's hatred for Geneviève?

A little ink rose into his blue eyes.

"Madame," he said, "you're right; the only guilty party in all of this is me—guilty of getting carried away, as

I was. As for what you have just said about Geneviève, listen to me carefully. The most beautiful book in the world is not worth a tiny corner of her smile. Even if she became one-eyed, infirm, stupid and malevolent I would still love her as on the first day. I will love her when she is old and I will love her when she is dead. I was eight years old when I understood that."

"I know that!" she said, in an almost mocking tone.

Charles-Étienne sat down and took his forehead in his hand.

"Madame," he ordered, raising his head, "you sit down too. I think that it is necessary to tell you the great secret of our childhood. That stained-glass window that you saw in the church . . ."

She listened to the fairy tale, her chin on her two palms; and all the Egypt of the great past, terrifying and sacred, was in her absolutely fixed eyes.

"Thank you," she said, in her most somber voice, when he had finished. "You have enabled me to understand many things." She fell silent for a moment, and resumed, so quietly that he could hardly hear her: "Geneviève has a double in the church. She can, therefore, change with impunity and grow old. We know that, my children, even better than you."

She stood up with those singular words. He saw her, tall and straight, head slowly for the door and go out without another word.

That evening, having sent word that she was ill, she did not appear at table.

XVIII

CHARLET persists in retaining a crestfallen expression. Yesterday evening, he asked for his pardon, and obtained it from a sad Geneviève, disdainful enough, then tender in her fashion, then amused and then irritated

"Good! That's all right. In any case, I understand your anger. It's quite natural."

This morning, she shrugs her shoulders around the familial milky coffee.

"You don't know, Father, and you, Uncle, that there are three children in the house instead of two. Look at the face he's pulling! Come on, be serious! Is there any news of the princess? Did she sleep well? Is she feeling better?"

"I don't know whether she slept well," grumbles old Bellecour, "but I was woken up by the dogs. What was the matter with them, to make such a racket?"

"Oh, you heard them too? And the children?"

"Me, yes," says Charles-Étienne. "I hadn't closed an eye when ..."

"Remorse?" she interrogates, mocking. "I slept so well that I didn't hear anything."

"I wondered whether there were prowlers around the house . . ." the uncle recommences.

The conversation stops there. The cook hurtles into the dining room, her lips trembling.

"The church was burgled last night! The stained-glass window is broken!"

Everyone stands up, Livid, Charles-Étienne repeats like an echo: "The stained-glass window is broken!"

With one bound he throws himself upon his wife.

"Geneviève . . . ! Geneviève . . . !"

She pushes him away gently. Her mouth is white.

"Let's go see . . ." she murmurs.

The little troupe only swelled the assembly of the village. In the midst of the people the curé, little, bald and very young, rolled his eyes fearfully.

"An acknowledged marvel . . . !" he repeated.

And all eyes looked on the ground, at the multicolored debris of Sainte Radegonde, fallen on to the flagstones and scattered on a few benches, in the place of whom a shapeless hole allowed the sight of the passing clouds.

"And they must have stolen everything in the church!" cried Monsieur de Bellecour.

"No, nothing, nothing!" stammered the unfortunate curé. "It's incomprehensible. It's the stained-glass window that they attacked."

"The wretches!" said Jean Masserand.

"It's a crime!" Geneviève emphasized.

And the crowd repeated with her, stormily: "It's a crime!"

Only Charles-Étienne said nothing.

The return to Beautilleul was a return from a burial. No one said anything. Charles-Étienne, still very pale, squeezed Geneviève's arm while walking, until it hurt. From time to time he looked at her with superstitious eyes.

As they went into the house, he whispered in her ear, through clenched teeth: "I love you . . ."

She was not astonished. The visage she showed him was as if illuminated by gratitude.

"Thank you!" she breathed.

They understood one another without explanations. It was something of Geneviève that had just disappeared, the transparent figure that, throughout their long amour, had never ceased to be mingled with her human figure. Almost humbly, she drew even closer to her husband.

"Perhaps I'm going to die . . ."

"Shut up! Shut up! My love will save you from anything!"

"Oh, Charles-Étienne . . . !"

They exchanged another gaze before going into the house. They had the sentiment that they had just cele-brated their marriage for the second time: a marriage that nothing could ever destroy.

Charles-Étienne could not obtain the miracle from himself of disguising his hatred until dusk, having as little control over his face as an impulsive child.

Antigone, who reappeared at lunch time with the plaintive expression requisite after her indisposition, was welcomed by this statement, which he hurled at her without even saying bonjour: "You know that the stained-glass window was broken last night?"

Her amazement was such that he began to doubt himself. All the voices recounted together, even Geneviève's. If she had known!

How sure her instinct was when we showed Sainte Radegonde to that somber madwoman! Geneviève carefully refrained from revealing the secret of our childhood!

A tragic agitation filled the house, the village and the surrounding area. The regional gendarmerie was mobilized, the first journalists arrived, and the crowd around the church grew.

When they got up from the table the princess said: "I'd like to go see too."

"Let's all go back," proposed Jean Masserand, sadly.

The part of the church where the glass had been broken had now been surrounded by an improvised barrier that kept the curious at a distance. That was already an officialization of the catastrophe, the commencement of the judiciary action, chilled horror. A gendarme was standing guard.

While Geneviève turned her head away, gripped by frissons at that sight, Charles-Étienne, stopped by the barrier, leaned toward Princess Antinides and whispered, looking into her eyes: "You don't have any cuts on your hands, Madame?"

She did not blink under his gaze. He was frightened by the natural tone in which she replied: "But I haven't yet tried to pick up any of the pieces as a souvenir. Why should I have cuts on my hands? To begin with, the gendarme would prevent me, wouldn't he?"

Until this evening, he thought. *All the same, you won't win the last round!*

All day long, he remained close to Geneviève, as if to protect her from an evil spell. Enclosed in their room, they abandoned the children to the nurse and the princess to their two parents.

At dinner, with a prodigious effort not to let anything appear:

"This misfortune ought not to prevent us from working, Madame. What do you say to resuming our classification? You don't go to bed before midnight, nor do I. So..."

"Agreed," she acquiesced, mildly.

Without waiting for her to sit down at the work table he marched straight toward her and, his jaw protruding and his eyes hard, he cried: "It's you who broke the window!"

Forcefully she replied: "Yes, it was me!"

Three seconds to register that frightful cynicism; then, breathlessly: "You hoped to break my love at the same time, but know this: even broken, the window is still there, because it's Geneviève that I love and not her image. Your magic can't succeed any more than your shameful provocations. I regret everything I owe to you. You're a wretch."

He recoiled before what he saw. Transfigured, the princess extended her hands to him.

"Thank you!"

"I don't understand you!" he declared, in the most scornful tone. Then, green with anger: "Not only have you tried to attack Geneviève, but you had no fear of destroying a pure masterpiece."

At the little laugh she uttered he started.

"That window wasn't a pure masterpiece. It has been repaired more than twenty times in various epochs. I can tell you which. I examined it carefully the other day."

"Really? And what permits you to advance that? How do you know it?"

"As I know all things."

There was terror in Charles-Étienne's low-pitched inflection. "In sum, who are you, then?"

She closed her eyes, showing her most beautiful face of death. Her lips scarcely moved. "I'm the eternal lady."

He could almost believe that she fainted on those words, for she tottered and fell on to the small divan behind her. She did not remain prostrate for long, however; her upper body straightened.

"Look carefully at this ring," she said, advancing her right hand. "It represents all of my long destiny."

He shuddered. The story of the Duc de Chables had just traversed his memory in a flash.

Meanwhile, she continued: "Charles-Étienne, you are the man for whom I have been searching for centuries."

He shrugged his shoulders furiously. "Good!" he muttered. "The madness is recommencing!"

With a perfectly calm movement, she shook her head. "I'm not mad, Charles-Étienne. I never have been."

He looked at her as she extended her arms toward him, but her gesture was so tender and so modest that he was moved in spite of himself.

"Please hear me out, and try to understand. I was searching for you, after all the amours I have had, but it was *for me* that I was searching for you, and not for another. Alas, alas! You are the only man I love, that I have ever truly loved, because you are the only man who is able to love. But it isn't me that you love."

He said "No!" with all his energy of a furious child, and she had the courage to smile at it.

"I know that full well, I know it only too well! Yes, it's Geneviève that you love, and you love her for herself and not for you, as you've declared since the first days in Alexandria. I didn't want to believe it, because I have never encountered that on my interminable route. I thought, therefore, that it didn't exist. But it exists, since here you are. It has required centuries of centuries for me to encounter you. I know: you continue to believe that I'm mad. But if you have the patience to listen to me, I'll tell you my life—or rather, my lives. You'll then learn how it is—you've asked me the question several times— how it is that I know everything, how I possess in Egypt the treasures that you've seen . . .

174

"Do you remember the old Duc de Chables falling unconscious at my feet? He believed me to be the great-granddaughter of the Belkis Effendi of his youth. The resemblance was so striking, wasn't it? And then, the ring . . . the ring he recognized on my finger, the ring whose imprint he bears on his temple. Of course, Belkis Effendi is me. Chables has grown old, as you all do, but I have retained my age. I have been thirty for more than three thousand years."

A limitless despair, of which Charles-Étienne had sometimes seen reflections in that beautiful exotic face, appeared this time without constraint, distressing her features.

"You're going to know all of my secret tonight, therefore. I have never spoken it while I have been breathing on this monotonous earth. Oh, listen to me without hatred and without dread, Charles-Étienne! Certainly, I have been criminal many times in the course of the centuries. I have killed men, I have killed women. I won't hide that from you. But as for who Geneviève is, I have never been anything but beneficial to her. You love her with the true amour, and I love you with the true amour. It's necessary, then, to conserve her, is it not? Everything that I know of the occult, I have used to safeguard her. Do you believe that I haven't saved her more than once, delicate as she is? What I have attempted that seems to be against her was to acquire the proof that your love for her was truly the one for which I was searching.

"I wanted to tempt you on the night that you remember, and you resisted. What dolor and what joy for me! What even greater dolor and joy when both of you pardoned me! She was very sure of you, Geneviève, incessantly to leave you alone with me, just at the moment when she was giving birth. A fine sum of disdain for me on the part of both of you! And yet, I am more dangerous than the most dangerous! You can say that you have enabled me to expiate all my cruelties, once and for all. Humiliated, me...?

"Then I tried to depoeticize Geneviève in your eyes. I haven't succeeded. You will never know the horrible anguish that your anger against her the other day caused me. For an instant, you gave the impression of being disgusted with her. If so, it would have been easy for me to triumph, and my triumph would have been the end of your amour—a triumph, yes, but a terrible defeat. And when you had told me the story of the window, with what terror I destroyed it, the double that might perhaps have explained esoterically your marvelous fidelity. But no! You love! You love her! *Alleluia*, then, and *de profundis!* I can die! I can die! Oh, if you suspected what that cry of deliverance is for me!"

His eyebrows furrowed, he was becoming weary of trying to follow her. He disentangled from the meanders of that thought so many tremulous revelations, a kind of logic so tightly-bound that it was no longer possible for him to shrug his shoulders. She threw one of the cushions on which she was leaning to the other end of the divan.

"Go on, sit down! You're going to hear everything. My hour has come. If you knew what is happening tonight!"

He obeyed, intrigued and perplexed, his heart hammering; he sensed that for several hours he was about to hear that tragic creature divagating, without taking his eyes off her.

The house was asleep, devoured by silence, in the autumn prey to darkness, through which a gust of wind sometimes passed. His face ardently extended toward her, Charles-Étienne listened to the demented secret of the eternal lady.

XIX

HE reports her words thus in the book that he consecrated to her a few years after her death.

At Elephantine, where I was born during the reign of the first Amenophis, I was a priestess in the temple of Hathor, my redoubtable sovereign.

I have already told you, beloved, what our rites and ceremonies of Hai Kouphta[1] were in the temples. I have told you as if I had studied it in books—or, rather, in the documents in my museum. But it is in my memory that I found all those absolutely unknown details, which have made you the king of Egyptology since your first book appeared. It is to you that I wanted to give the treasures of my memory, in the same way that, before opening it to everyone, I delivered to you alone the secrets of my crypt, the poor residue of my riches, preserved with so much

---

1 Presumably a reference to the festival of Anuket, the goddess of the cataracts of the Nile, held at the end of the month of Hathor at Elephantine.

difficulty from all the destructions that have unfurled over Misraim.[1]

My name as a priestess was Amanit—yes, the same one that my yacht bears, about which you interrogated me, do you remember? My true name only my parents knew, for you also know as well as I do that a name is a being and that it is necessary to preserve that being from the emprise of others by hiding it. I know that name, my own, but I have never revealed it and never will reveal it, even to you, for our ritual forbids it. It will therefore die with me, very soon, I would like to hope.

The high priest of my temple conceived a sacrilegious amour for the officiant that I was. One day, when the two of us were alone in the temple, preparing a ceremony for the night, he dared to declare that amour to me, which I had already perceived, not without extreme displeasure—for, apart from the offense made to the gods, he was no longer young, and my heart did not speak for him, nor my senses of a young virgin.

As I listened to him, trembling with fear, he seized me in his arms and, having struck me in order to vanquish my resistance, he possessed me, half-unconscious, at the feet of the goddess. When I opened my eyes again, I saw him at prayer, and tears inundated his curly beard. He believed that he had killed me, and was begging the gods to resuscitate me.

---

1 Misraim is the Hebrew name for Egypt, also found in Babylonian texts; its use by Antigone seems odd, but Delarue-Mardrus would have been familiar with the scholarly fantasies of the French Occult Revival, various offshoots of which made much of the imaginary "Ancient and Primitive rite of Memphis and Misraim," sometimes abbreviated to "the Misraim rite."

I gathered my strength and, taking advantage of his ecstasy, I delivered a mortal blow to his head with one of the heavy bronze vases that served for the sacrifices.

I remained stupefied and trembling before his bloody body when Isis herself was manifest.

We knew when the great goddess was manifest by virtue of a light that enveloped us and the terror into which we entered.

I had just committed an inexpiable crime by soiling the altar with the blood of the high priest.

Prostrate, I awaited death. The words of the divinity reached me as they reached us in those times that are no more. Our ears did not hear them, but only our minds.

"Your condemnation is not death, but worse than death. You will no longer find repose until the day when you encounter the sole true amour, since it is because of a sacrilegious amour that your crime has been committed. On that day, open the golden ring that you wear on your finger as a priestess. The talisman that it contains, I am investing with a new power. It will deliver you, when the time has come, from the condemnation of the gods.

"Keep this sentence secret until the day when you are delivered; if not, execration and woe be upon you!

"Now go! Seek the man who loves truly, and whom you will love truly; seek your salvation on this earth."

I got up from my prostration. The Presence was no longer there. Without having understood the meaning of the fatal edict, I fled the temple and fled Elephantine, on foot, incessantly expecting to be overtaken by the royal guard—for, on discovering the murdered high priest, they would certainly not fail to accuse me, with good reason, of his death, since I was alone in the temple with him.

I will not recount to you all the episodes of that flight, the first voyage that I accomplished overland. Only know that, having ended up settling in a poor village in the Delta, begging in order to live, more wretched than the most wretched, without news of my rich and noble family, for whom I was nothing henceforth but a dead person, I was loved by a poor fisherman, who, believing me to be of the same class as himself, sad beggar that I was, married the stranger recently arrived in his country and enabled her to share his life of toil and privations.

I had invented a story regarding my origins that I told everyone—the first of many stories, which was to be followed by thousands of others, but I did not know that yet.

It seemed to me that I was expiating my crime by accepting the sordid life and the humble companion that destiny offered me, and I did my utmost, virtuously, to be a docile, courageous and faithful wife. My first youth had been succeeded by the plenitude of my beauty, which was recognized to be great by all those who saw me, although they were only of the lowest class of people.

That beauty, for which I had first been violated, earned me the hatred of women, the amour of men and the jealousy of my husband—which is to say, many torments, many curses and many blows.

Resigned to my unhappy fate, since I was paying a debt, I told myself, in order to console me, that old age would not take long to liberate me from so much suffering. I was then thirty years old, as I seem to be today.

Leaning over the Nile marshes, as if over the fragments of a great mirror, I tried to perceive in the water the appearance of the first gray hairs that would have announced the commencement of my deliverance, but it was necessary, at length, to take account of the truth. The years passed, my companion became white-haired and stooped, all the contemporaries who surrounded me gradually displayed on their faces the signs of age, which resemble the scars of a profound wound—a profound wound indeed, since it is that of time, of which one dies. I alone did not age.

The man who had married me was sixty years old, then seventy, and then eighty. Those who had prowled around my youth were only old men, like him. The women who had resented me, now toothless grandmothers, no longer cared about anything but their infirmities. Slender, splendid and healthy, I had not surpassed by a single day the thirty terrifying years about which the astonished village had been murmuring for a long time.

I waited for the death of my husband, for whom I cared devotedly until the end, in order to disappear again, sensing that my presence, having become supernatural, was no longer possible among the new generation that was growing up alongside me.

I commenced, alas, to understand my punishment.

I returned, as you will understand, to Elephantine. It was to find that all my relatives were dead, save for my grandmother, who recognized me in spite of her great age and mistook me for her great-granddaughter, the child of the woman who had disappeared. A second invention on my part aided her in her illusion. I was the unique heir to my family's great wealth. With intoxication, I rediscovered the luxury and the high culture of my caste.

Among all those who loved me, a prince came to please me. I believed that I loved him, and that he loved me. Our marriage was celebrated with the greatest sumptuousness. I had, therefore, after a life of misery, found the repose promised by the gods. I tried to open the ring—this one, which I no longer had to hide, and was able to wear on my finger overtly—in order to expose the talisman of Isis, but I could not succeed. Divine power prevented me from doing so. I understood that it was necessary to wait again, and shortly afterwards, the succession of events showed me that, in fact, the time had not yet come.

I had quit the poorest and most ignorant class, and gradually, in the most fortunate and the most learned, I rediscovered exactly the same manifestations that had made me suffer so much in my hovel in the Delta: the amorous men, the hateful women, the jealous husband, the curses, and the blows.

I took advantage of the departure of my princely spouse, summoned by a war, to reside in my own palace, the one that came to me from my family; and after having walled up the subterrains crammed with riches, in which my own sarcophagus awaited me, I set fire to the vast domain and, assumed to be dead and calcined in the general conflagration, I fled Elephantine for a second time, going to live elsewhere the unalterable youth that I knew now to be my bitter punishment. Alas, I was condemned to life as others are condemned to death.

To find the man who loves truly and whom I would love truly, I thought, might perhaps be easy in other regions.

Friend, need I tell you that I traveled all of the Egypt of those canonical times, saw dynasties succeeding dynasties, wars succeeding wars, poverty succeeding prosperity and prosperity poverty . . . that I tried all the classes of the societies that succeeded one another in the land of my birth, knew all amours and all execrations, and thought many a time that I would be able to open the ring, without succeeding, because the same joys followed the same troubles monotonously, forming a sequence in the course of my tortuous and tortured youth?

After several centuries I had almost acquired the habitude of cruelty and crime. Without waiting for their ferocity, I simply suppressed those who loved me, and even those I loved—or thought I loved—before they had time to manifest their passion by means of ill-treatment, tragedy or other signs of the monstrous tyranny known as amour.

From one century to another, faithfully, I returned to Elephantine and visited my crypts, then unlimited—for you have only seen a poor vestige of what I once possessed. My family was no more than those rows of sarcophagi over which you cast a rapid glance some time ago, for the hypogeum, my sole link with this world, is still intact, as you have observed. And in each of my voyages, for three thousand years, I have been able to visit my house of eternity and honor my own sepulcher in accordance with the protocol of my caste.

To get back to those early lives, a day came when, weary even of my homeland, I wanted to attempt new lands, and I embarked for Greece.

I cannot tell you everything; we only have one night before us. In any case, the sequence is of scant importance. Only know that my imperishable youth continued through the ages and the civilizations.

In Greece I was by turns a courtesan, a philosopher, a prostitute in Piraeus, a virtuous lady in a gynaeceum. I saw the decadence of Athens, and the torch of the world passed into the hands of Rome. I went quite naturally toward that Roman light. I knew the brothels and the palaces of Latinity, the gladiators and the Caesars; I continued traveling, always in search of the impossible thing that the mocking gods had given me as a goal and a deliverance. I was in Judea at the commencement of your era and, without paying any great attention to him, I saw your Christ pass by in the midst of his verminous followers—remember my stool signed by his hand . . . and you were astonished that I knew Hebrew.

In between times I sometimes returned to my Egypt, out of filial love and to draw upon my reserves of gold. It became a Macedonian province under Alexander the Great, and then Greek. I knew Cleopatra personally! After Rome had intervened in the affairs of Ptolemy V, Egypt was a Roman province. Previously, it had been Assyrian and Persian and had vomited all of that, because, since the Hyksos, my fatherland, fundamentally, has never admitted foreigners, even while submitting to them. It had its highs and its lows, but it was always great. Do you know that it was Necho,[1] in fact, who commenced the Suez Canal?

I went back there to observe, dolorously, the thefts committed in my subterranean treasures and the changes brought by the foreigner. Cleopatra, although Greek, was to be the last figure still aureoled by the light of Isis. In entering into Roman history the land of the Pharaohs had to lose the most mysterious element of its prestige.

Was not the Emperor Marcian—permit me to laugh with rage!—in the early years of your era, forced by the Blemmyes, the ancestors of the Bichari who still reside in our south, to recognize for a further hundred years the cult of Isis? A hundred years . . . she who had reigned for millennia![2]

But all that ought no longer to scandalize me. My sarcophagus awaits me, behind the little golden door that I showed you . . .

Under Nero, Egypt had commenced becoming Christian. And I too have been Christian, you will not doubt. In Rome I was delivered to the lions. I knew that they would not touch me, did I not?

Oh, I'm fatigued by all that I'm telling you. Think . . . ! To have lived all that!

---

1 Necho II (610-595 B.C.) was said by Herodotus to have undertaken numerous major construction projects, including a canal intended to facilitate trade between the Mediterranean and the Indian Ocean.

2 Marcian was emperor of the Eastern Roman Empire from 450-457, in a period of violent wars, intense theological disputes and the persecution of heresies. In a peace treaty that he concluded with the Blemmyes he conceded then access to the temple of Isis at Philae, thus sparing it from conversion to a Christian church, for a hundred years.

I must certainly pass over all my avatars; one cannot remember everything . . . and what would be the point? It was always the same story in other costumes and under other reigns. What do I know? I was a Byzantine princess in the third Carthage, an Arab sultana disguised as a man and leading hordes, a slave in the times of Saint Louis' crusades, brought back to France to be a lady of his court presiding over tourneys. I have been a scullion in the kitchens of Anne de Beaujeu, imprisoned for life in Norway; then I was a witch in Paris, condemned to be burned; I departed over the sea; I have lived in India, as a pariah or a princess; I was in Italy at the commencement of the Renaissance . . . oh, my stories of Venice, if you knew! Perhaps I have never been poisoned so frequently by people as in that epoch! In the time of Henry VII, I was a nun in an English convent. Under Henri V, King of France and Navarre, I was an inn servant in the Midi. Under Louis XII, I was a fabricator of venomous make-up, under Louis XIV a boyaress in Russia, under Louis XV a lady of the Polish court, received at Versailles, yes, in the Hall of Mirrors. Under Louis XVI, I was a Revolutionary and wore the red bonnet in the streets of Paris. Under the Directoire I was a dancer and courtesan in Spain, and then the wife of a chieftain on the South America pampas; under Louis-Philippe a quakeress in North America. Under Napoléon I, I was a German spy, under Napoléon III—ah, we're finally arriving—I was a Turkish adventuress, that Belkis Effendi who left the mark of her ring on the temple of your Duc de Chables. And always, Elephantine saw me again. It was there that I accumulated in the cellars that you didn't see . . . oh, what documents of universal history!

And today, I am the Princess Antinides whom you see, the inconsolable widow who poisoned her prince in India by means of the plague, once her palace was reconstructed.

The story that Prince Ahmed believes and relates is my last invention, thank God!

And *voilà!* through all of that, my child, the one thing that I wanted to be able to show you, is amour, always amour, and always the frightful egotism of amour. The millions of men that I have known in all latitudes and in all times have been the same. They have beaten me, tormented me, and imprisoned me; they have tried to kill me, they have done worse: they have made scenes because I was young and beautiful, and they have loved me. And I have loved no better than them; I have deceived, tortured and killed them. You know the tombs that I visited in Alexandria? Three of my most recent victims—only three; I can no longer even calculate their number.

Now, here you are beside me on this poor little rustic divan, you who are only your age, and you are my deliverance, finally, because it is you that I love and because it is you who love. I love you enough to have wanted your happiness before mine, and it is the first time in so many centuries. For a long time, I would have made your Geneviève die the most natural death . . . on the contrary, I have protected her, as I have told you—me, who, has known no rivals or, if I sometimes knew them, made them disappear at the first sign. I have found you. I love you. And you love truly, since everything that I have done to tempt you has not succeeded.

Oh, with what desire for you and what terror of seeing you succumb I offered you my beauty, my eternal youth, on that terrible night! If you had yielded, I would have had the happiness of finally possessing you, but it would also have been my fall and the disappointment of all my hope. For then you would no longer have been the man who loves truly, the lover of a single and unique woman, inaccessible to foreign seduction, and I would have had to pursue my frightful eternity, to recommence searching for that man. What a dilemma! What a combat in my heart between my amour for Charles-Étienne and my desire for death! Oh, Geneviève, if you knew that it requires three thousand years to discover a Charles-Étienne ... !

I love you ... you love Geneviève. I'm redeemed. I shall go to lie down in my sarcophagus in Elephantine, which has been waiting for me for three thousand years. The ring will open under my fingers, Isis will be manifest, I shall fold my arms and I shall fall asleep in death. I shall not have, like my ancestors lying around me, the honors of seventy ritual days in the bath of natron, I shall not be injected and garnished with aromatics, crammed with amulets and statuettes, charged with jewels and surrounded by figurines. I shall not be a mummy; I shall not have respondents, but I am so weary of breathing that I do not wish the Ka to continue to live in my body, or my double to cultivate the fields of Ialou. No priest will blow into my mouth in order to make an Osiris of my cadaver. I shall do without preparation, I shall not be anointed with the sacred oil, I shall not be gilded in the face and the hands, perfumed, wrapped in linen, rolled in bandages, and enveloped in a painted shroud; I shall not be boxed, sheathed in a coffin ornamented with magical paintings, but I shall be laid in my first class sarcophagus alongside my relatives, in the sevenfold familial darkness, and thus I shall not be completely in breach of the ritual of my only religion—I, Amanit, priestess of Hathor!

Now, give me your two hands, that I might press them one last time, and be happy with your amour. And when, one day, you know that everything I have said to you tonight was not the dementia that you still believe it to be, but the truth, you might think of the dead woman that I shall finally be, in spite of all her crimes, with some tenderness. And Khaibit, my great black shadow, will continue to watch over you, over your companion, and over your children.

I love you. Adieu forever!

EPILOGUE

A little more than a year after that phantasmagorical night and the clandestine departure of Antigone at dawn, as Charles-Étienne and Geneviève, after having written ten times, were anxious at remaining without news, they were astounded to receive in Paris a letter from a notary in Paris informing them of the formidable legacy that had been left to them by Princess Antinides.

They went pale.

"She's dead, then?"

An instant later, Jean Masserand hurtled into their room, a newspaper in his hand. "The Antinides palace in Elephantine has burned down. Princess Antinides must have perished in the flames."

A feverish agitation took possession of Charles-Étienne. He remembered, among other things, the episode recounted by the madwoman on that unforgettable night: "I set fire to the vast domain and, assumed to be dead and calcined in the general conflagration, I fled Elephantine for a second time."

Had she made a prediction in believing that she was recounting her past?

Geneviève, to whom he had recounted everything, as always, said: "Let's not worry too much, Charlet! You'll see that she'll reappear abruptly. After this great coup—for its probable that she is the arsonist; one can suppose that after seeing what she did to the stained-glass window in Beautilleul—she must have gone to seek treatment again, and she'll return to us cured . . . for a while. Her legacy, which we can't accept, is another folly, be sure of it."

However, a second letter from the notary came to aggravate their presentiments, at the same time as the daily newspapers commented on the event. Everything was affirmed. The princess really had died in the flames, even though nothing of her had yet been recovered from the rubble. Fortunately, being subterranean, her magnificent museum, open for some time, had not suffered.

Heirs, in spite of themselves, to an immense fortune, Charles-Étienne and Geneviève were making their final preparations a month later to go to Egypt. Given what they knew about their friend, they wanted to carry out a discreet investigation into her disappearance.

They thought, not without disturbance, about the hypogeum that Charles-Étienne had seen, the existence of which no one else suspected. Did they have the right to reveal poor Antinides' secret.

"What if she isn't dead?" said Genevieve, obstinately. "She's always been mysterious. God only knows in what retreat she's hiding. Let's be patient. I still have the idea that she'll come back."

"In the meantime, our voyage to Egypt is necessary, isn't it?"

"Certainly. Anyway, if only because of your second book, it's a voyage to be made."

"My second book . . . without her, it's necessary that I live on the notes, fortunately complete, that she dictated to me. But she would have connected them up with such precision . . . that's why the hypogeum . . ."

"Since you remember the place so well, we'll be able to find it easily."

"Difficult . . . she alone knew the enigma of those doors, those stairways and those dead ends. And if she isn't dead, we can't even try to . . ."

They were at that point when there was a second *coup de théâtre* in the press.

An Englishman has discovered, near to the ruins of the Antinides palace, the entrance to a hypogeum that seems to be in a perfect state of conservation. The Egyptology of the entire world is en route *to the marvel.*

"Too late!" groaned Charles-Étienne. "We should have departed earlier and set our scruples aside. We've been anticipated!

"But if she's alive, she'll be able to forbid the theft of her property in time."

"Oh, if she's alive! She promised me . . ."

"You're only thinking about your book. However, we're millionaires now, thanks to her! Personally, it's her I'm thinking about!"

"Me too. But you understand, Egyptology, science . . ."

"Are you becoming ingrate, Charles-Étienne?"

He shuddered, and then lowered his head profoundly.

"You're right, Geneviève . . . it's necessary to pardon me."

※

The trunks are packed, the seat booked on the train and the steamer. The thunderbolt arrives.

Hypogeum opened . . . cadaver of a woman in decomposition in one of the sarcophagi . . . a matter of a recent death.

The newspaper fell from Charles-Étienne's hands. The blood retreated from his veins, he gazed at his wife and murmured: "She announced all this to me on the night of her adieux . . ."

His blue eyes widened. In a breath, his hand clenched over his mouth, traversed by a frightful thought:

"But in that case . . . ?"

Even more imperceptibly, he continued, ashamed and terrified by what he dared to proffer:

"Perhaps, Geneviève . . . perhaps everything that she told me . . . ?"

AFTERWORD

IT is probably not a coincidence that *Amanit* was published a year after *My First Two Thousand Years: The Autobiography of the Wandering Jew* (1928) by George Sylvester Viereck and Paul Eldridge, although the latter book was not translated into French and Lucie Delarue-Mardrus is highly unlikely to have read it. She would certainly have known George Viereck's name, however, as he was one of the most famous journalists in the world, and she might conceivably have met him in Paris during one of his numerous trips to Europe, perhaps in Paris in 1904-8, when he was a conspicuously Decadent poet extremely fond of the work of Oscar Wilde, and unafraid to introduce homosexual themes into his own literary endeavors. At any rate, she was probably aware of the existence of *My First Two Thousand Years*—a sensational best-seller in America—and the bare bones of its plot: the central character, condemned to expiatory immortality by Jesus, employs his time in an endless quest to discover the "secret" of "unendurable pleasure indefinitely prolonged."

Viereck and Edridge went on to produce a sequel to their novel with a female protagonist, *Salome: the Wandering Jewess* (1930), but Delarue-Mardrus could not have known that in 1929 and would probably not have approved of the assertions of that novel regarding the fundamental nature of female psychology, although, if the lightly-disguised representation of her husband in the first version of Renée Vivien's quasi-autobiographical *Une Femme m'apparut* (1904) is reliable, he had held a very similar opinion, justified by a similar psychoanalytical argument. Delarue-Mardrus' depiction of a woman condemned to expiatory immortality is a very different counterpart to Viereck and Eldridge's Cartaphilus, not in quest of the ultimate orgasm but of the "secret" of true amour, something assumed from the outset to be far rarer than unicorns, because all men are brutes.

The plot of the novella conscientiously leaves open the possibility, of course, that Antigone is not really the eternal Lady Amanit at all, but merely a madwoman who happens to have inherited a secret museum of Egyptian antiquities from a husband who died of the plague. Perhaps that is a sop to readers possessed of an unfortunately-common allergy to the supernatural, but it is not impossible that it is a transfiguration of aspects of the author's own self-doubt; in either case, it is only marginally relevant to the philosophical questions raised and addressed by her quest. After all, the one-sided dialogues between the author's alter egos and two different Amanits in the 1911 and 1923 stories are perfectly imaginary, but the argumentative points they make are real, and certainly seemed genuinely relevant to the author.

In both earlier cases, the author's alter ego identifies imaginatively with an ancient Egyptian "sister" while in quest of some insight into her own existential situation; writing the stories was presumably an aspect of the same quest, which is surely carried forward in *Amanit*, with the usual cryptic disguise that writing fiction provides for its practitioners. *Amanit* is a markedly different literary exercise, employing an objective narrative voice to study from without, as it were, a character who fuses the author with the undead mummy by means of an alchemy of which only imaginative literature is capable, but the existential questions at stake therein are essentially similar to those raised in the short stories.

When Delarue-Mardrus wrote *Amanit* she was fifty-four years old, and her meteoric career as a "professional beauty" was far behind her. The fear of growing old expressed in some of her early short stories and brought into sharp focus in "La Princesse en balade" had been realized, which must have added an extra piquancy to the fantasy of imagining how things might have been if she could have stopped aging at thirty and remained a professional beauty forever. But Princesse Patricia's imaginary psychiatric consultation with the real Amanit had a broader context than the erosion of her looks, and the massive sulk that sent her away from Paris to revisit various locations of her earlier tourism was a more deep-seated disenchantment with life's possibilities and rewards. In 1911, when "La Princesse en balade" was written, Delarue-Mardrus was still married, but the marriage was, as the conventional phrase has it "on the rocks," having apparently followed a common trajectory from disappointing unfulfillment to frank intolerability.

Exactly why Delarue-Mardrus found amour so woefully unfulfilling is impossible to determine, but appearances suggest that she did not find it much more enduring or ultimately satisfactory in lesbian relationships than in heterosexual ones. As Antigone argues, the answer to the riddle of the sphinx is the fundamental essence of human nature: the antagonism between the head and the rump, the intellect and the sexual impulse. But *Amanit* is a devil's advocate of a book, which deliberately posits that, however unlikely it might be, true love must be possible, and asks the further question: if it were possible, what would it look like? And it is the hypothetical answer that the story-line provides that makes the story truly bizarre.

The supernatural hypothesis of the text is frankly insane—the verdict and sentence issued by Isis are even more ridiculous than the sentence and verdict delivered by Jesus on the legendary Wandering Jew—but it is surely more plausible, in esthetic terms, than the assertions that, if ever there were to be a man capable of true love, it would be someone like Charles-Étienne Masserand, and that the inevitable object of his amour would be someone like Genevière Le Rieux.

Could any reader really believe for an instant, without the authority of the text, that Antigone, who has a vast spectrum of comparison, would even spare an ineffectual wimp like Charles-Étienne a second glance, let alone fall in love with him? And could any reader believe for an instant, even with that authority, that the stubbornness of Charles-Étienne's amorous loyalty to the absurdly perverse Geneviève is anything but a pathological compulsion devoid of any logic or moral entitlement—the result of an arbitrary supernatural thunderbolt for which he has no moral or intellectual responsibility?

Perhaps, however, that is the whole point; after all, the truly great lovers of French history are not the imaginary Tristan and Iseult, hypothetical inventions of pure Romance, but the castrate Abelard and the lachrymose Héloïse, whose emotional obstinacy would surely have been impossible had they actually been able to have sex, marry and raise children. None of the great love stories of French literature has a "happy ending," and seen collectively, they surely endorse the tacit conviction of Delarue-Mardrus' world-view: that amour is merely ironically suspended tragedy, that the best thing of all is not to fall victim to it, and the second best to get it over with as quickly as possible.

In what passes for "real" life in the story, Antigone's neurotic mourning for her once-beloved prince is a fake, according to her own testimony, and she actually poisoned him by infecting him with the plague. We cannot know what Lucie Delarue-Mardrus thought about her ex-husband in 1929, sixteen years after their divorce, but writing a novel based in the Egyptology in which he had fancied himself a great expert must have stirred up relevant memories and feelings. Whatever the reasons for the peculiarity of her depiction of a love story with a "happy ending" might have been, however, one implication of the text is clear: the conviction that the eternalization of splendid female beauty could only result in its possessor becoming just as bad as the brutalizing males who make the life of such beauties unendurable.

There can be little doubt that it is Antigone rather than Geneviève who is the primary point of identification within the text for the author, but it is worth noting that the "eternal lady" only appears explicitly in the text at the very end; prior to that, she is a teasing enigmatic presence. She is not a focal point of identification for the reader—quite the contrary, in fact. The character offered to the reader for primary identification is Charles-Étienne, the imaginative child arbitrarily gifted with a purpose in life—which is to say, a helpful pathological obsession—by an explicitly religious revelation. From his viewpoint, Geneviève is just as enigmatic as Antigone, but is seen, thanks to a trick of the light and a dash of mood music, to be saintly rather than diabolical. The triumph of his "true" love for her is that it survives her gradual humanization, as she not only condescends—albeit very belatedly—to kiss him, but to have sex, bear children and run to fat. The ultimate proof of his fidelity, according to his own words, is the assertion that he would love her even if she were ugly, and will love her even when she is old; and the greatest proof of Antigone's gullibility is that she believes him, although that belief evidently has the endorsement of Isis, who allows her to kill herself without waiting for an evidential demonstration.

As to why Geneviève loves Charles-Étienne, we can only wonder; even though she does not have Antigone's opportunities for comparison, it seems a trifle odd. If Charles-Étienne is all that is on offer in a woefully depleted world, amour-wise, surely she, of all people ought to be able to do without, and to be content with avoidance? All three main characters are, in essence, insane, without much evidence of method in their madness—but then, so are we all, if the fundamental argument of the text and the Sphinx can be taken seriously; and who among us is sufficiently sane to cast the first critical stone in indignant denial?

The reader of *Amanit* has to accept, while imaginatively projected into the text, that the depiction of true love within it is accurate, because the author is its creator, and what the creator says goes. But when the text ends and the reader is cast back into awful reality, the invitation is there to ask questions. Is that really what true love is like? Is that really the only kind of true love that can exist in our corrupt world? The text, of course, only pretends to provide an answer, because texts are, by their nature, hypothetical; their role is not to provide answers but to illuminate questions. As a creator, Lucie Delarue-Mardrus could do anything within the imaginary worlds of her texts, but as a person living in the real world she had to put up with much the same existential restraints, confusions and perversities as everybody else. Did the explorations of her writing enable her to cope with them better than the unimaginative majority ordinarily seem to do? Who can tell? Can they help her readers? Perhaps—but at the very least, they provide food for thought, and perhaps a little nourishment independent of mere taste. That is why *Amanit*, because rather than in spite of its implausibility, is worth reading and pondering.

—Brian Stableford

FREDERICK ROLFE (**Baron Corvo**) *An Ossuary of the North Lagoon and Other Stories*
JASON ROLFE *An Archive of Human Nonsense*
ARNAUD RYKNER *The Last Train*
MARCEL SCHWOB *The Assassins and Other Stories*
MARCEL SCHWOB *Double Heart*
CHRISTIAN HEINRICH SPIESS *The Dwarf of Westerbourg*
BRIAN STABLEFORD (**editor**)
  Decadence and Symbolism: A Showcase Anthology
BRIAN STABLEFORD (**editor**) *The Snuggly Satyricon*
BRIAN STABLEFORD (**editor**) *The Snuggly Satanicon*
BRIAN STABLEFORD *Spirits of the Vasty Deep*
COUNT ERIC STENBOCK *Love, Sleep & Dreams*
COUNT ERIC STENBOCK *Myrtle, Rue & Cypress*
COUNT ERIC STENBOCK *The Shadow of Death*
COUNT ERIC STENBOCK *Studies of Death*
MONTAGUE SUMMERS *The Bride of Christ and Other Fictions*
MONTAGUE SUMMERS *Six Ghost Stories*
GILBERT-AUGUSTIN THIERRY *The Blonde Tress and The Mask*
GILBERT-AUGUSTIN THIERRY *Reincarnation and Redemption*
DOUGLAS THOMPSON *The Fallen West*
TOADHOUSE *Gone Fishing with Samy Rosenstock*
TOADHOUSE *Living and Dying in a Mind Field*
TOADHOUSE *What Makes the Wave Break?*
LÉO TRÉZENIK *Decadent Prose Pieces*
RUGGERO VASARI *Raun*
ILARIE VORONCA *The Confession of a False Soul*
JANE DE LA VAUDÈRE *The Demi-Sexes and The Androgynes*
JANE DE LA VAUDÈRE *The Double Star and Other Occult Fantasies*
JANE DE LA VAUDÈRE *The Mystery of Kama and Brahma's Courtesans*
JANE DE LA VAUDÈRE *Three Flowers and The King of Siam's Amazon*
JANE DE LA VAUDÈRE *The Witch of Ecbatana and The Virgin of Israel*
AUGUSTE VILLIERS DE L'ISLE-ADAM *Isis*
RENÉE VIVIEN AND HÉLÈNE DE ZUYLEN DE NYEVELT
  Faustina and Other Stories
RENÉE VIVIEN *Lilith's Legacy*
RENÉE VIVIEN *A Woman Appeared to Me*
ILARIE VORONKA *The Confession of a False Soul*
ILARIE VORONKA *The Key to Reality*
TERESA WILMS MONTT *In the Stillness of Marble*
TERESA WILMS MONTT *Sentimental Doubts*
KAREL VAN DE WOESTIJNE *The Dying Peasant*

www.ingramcontent.com/pod-product-compliance
Lightning Source LLC
Chambersburg PA
CBHW050327110726
47899CB00007B/2403